APPLIANCE

Natural Mechanical
Long Cuts
At Maldon
In Casting Off
Interference Pattern
Assurances
The Martian's Regress
Pupa

APPLIANCE

J. O. MORGAN

JONATHAN CAPE
LONDON

1 3 5 7 9 10 8 6 4 2

Jonathan Cape is part of the Penguin Random House group
of companies whose addresses can be found at
global.penguinrandomhouse.com.

Penguin
Random House
UK

© J. O. Morgan 2022

J. O. Morgan has asserted his right to be identified as the author of this
Work in accordance with the Copyright, Designs and Patents Act 1988

First published by Jonathan Cape in 2022

penguin.co.uk/vintage

A CIP catalogue record for this book is available from the British Library

ISBN 9781787333888

Typeset by the author
Printed and bound by TJ Books Ltd

The authorised representative in the EEA is Penguin Random House
Ireland, Morrison Chambers, 32 Nassau Street, Dublin DO2 YH68

Penguin Random House is committed to a sustainable future for
our business, our readers and our planet. This book is made from
Forest Stewardship Council® certified paper.

MIX
Paper from
responsible sources
FSC
www.fsc.org   FSC® C013056

and this is only the start of what they'll do,
soon nothing they propose will be beyond them

GENESIS 11:6

and with a quaint device
the banquet vanishes

THE TEMPEST 3:3

APPLIANCE

1. Bring it Inside

THE UNIT itself resembled nothing quite so much as a large grey refrigerator, an imposing foreign model, with one thick door below and one smaller above, each curved like the roof of a car and each with a long chrome handle; except that the lower handle was secured with a heavy padlock, and the upper handle was not to be touched unless the green light on top of the unit was lit. Because, quite unlike a refrigerator, the unit had an array of three small differently-coloured bulbs cresting its glossy top; and the weighty control box, bolted to the side of the unit, with its cold-cathode display and raised rubber keypad, was not a thermostat.

It was Friday evening when four well-dressed men from the institute arrived to angle and wheel and steady the machine on its trolley, out of their old blue van and up the garden path, to be inched through Mr Pearson's front door.

They took every care with this delicate operation. They were in no hurry. They checked and rechecked the dimensions of the open gate, tying the wrought iron back with garden twine. They examined the rough concrete of the path for dints and cracks. They laid long planks over the front steps. They wiped the sweat from their palms on cotton handkerchiefs. Then all four men held very tightly to the tall grey box as it was rolled up and into the house, as though to let it fall, even for it to be bumped or scratched, would be a catastrophe, would spell the end of the world.

Mr Pearson did not take part in proceedings other than to clear the hallway of likely obstacles while explaining to his wife that yes, they had indeed asked his permission, and that yes, he knew exactly what to expect and that he'd fill her in on the finer details in due course, once the unit was properly installed.

Mr Pearson did not work in the same department as these other men. Mr Pearson had been specially chosen. Mr Pearson and his wife were to be entrusted with this machine, this prototype, for just a few days, while certain basic tests were carried out. They would themselves take part in these tests. Mr Pearson had been issued with detailed instructions. Plus, in stark comparison to the many other employees, Mr Pearson lived reasonably close to the institute, and this it seemed made all the difference.

The unit came to a rest in the kitchen. There was no obvious place for it to stand so it jutted awkwardly into the middle of the room. It couldn't be set flush against the wall because of the stiff cabling that ran out from the back and because it was deemed sensible, at least for the test period, to keep all sides of the unit unobstructed and freely accessible. The singular cable was as thick as a baby's forearm and sheathed in soft brown rubber. It was screwed in place on the unit by way of a tough plastic collar, with the cable itself trailing from the kitchen, down the hall and on out through the front door's letterbox.

Having assessed the machine's stability, and having plugged its spindly power lead into the nearest wall socket, the four men departed, leaving Mr and Mrs Pearson to consider this new addition to their kitchen furniture.

An amber bulb glowed softly from the top of the unit. Mr Pearson didn't know quite what this signified but stood with his hands in his pockets, beaming at the machine.

Mrs Pearson stood behind him with her arms tightly folded. She did not smile.

'And what are we meant to do if we need to go out?'

'Hmm?' Mr Pearson did not take his eyes from the machine.

'And there'll be a fine draught too, what with that letterbox stuck open all night.'

Mr Pearson took a slow step back and sat down, still beaming.

'If this thing works like they say it will—' He wagged a finger at the cumbersome machine. 'My my. Well. Indeed. This is going to be something. Really something.'

Mrs Pearson sighed and sat down beside her husband.

'You never said this is what they were working on.'

'I didn't know a thing about it. Nobody knew. Not us lot in Personnel, at any rate. It's to be expected. The only thing we all know for sure is that we never really know what they're working on. And if by chance we ever get to know then we're sworn not to let anybody else know. I had to sign some sort of form to say so.'

'That's as may be.' Mrs Pearson glanced towards the kitchen window. 'But I never took such an oath. And now what am I to say when people ask about the unsightly cable sticking out our front door? Because they will ask. It goes right down the front path. And how much further on after that? Well, I imagine all the way to the institute, too. That's a good quarter of a mile, at least. There will be all sorts of gossip when folk see it coming right up into our house. And I'm no liar. I don't have the patience for it. So when they do ask—'

Mr Pearson got to his feet once again, his hands back in his pockets. He strolled slowly round the machine, examining it from every angle.

'They'll have that all figured out, I expect. All sorted.' He stooped to inspect the cable's connection point. He put out a hand to check the coupling was secure then remembered himself and drew back. 'They'll have put out some sort of notice. Spoken to those who need speaking to.' He waved his free hand dismissively, then returned it to his pocket. 'They'll have warning signs up. No tampering. Danger of death. Sizeable penalties. You needn't worry about anything. I'll wager you won't even be asked.'

His circuit complete, Mr Pearson came back to sit beside his wife. He opened his mouth to continue with his reassurances but at that moment something changed. The amber light on top of the unit winked out. One moment more and the red bulb came on.

Mr Pearson stood immediately, the knuckles of his fist against pursed lips. His wife, too, slowly rose to stand beside him.

For a while neither of them moved and nothing further happened with the machine. There had been no sound, no warning tone, just the languid shift from one bulb to the other, a soft red light now glowing on the two expectant faces.

After a while Mrs Pearson's shoulders sagged.

'Do you think that's it done, then?'

'Shh!' Her husband motioned sharply with his hand.

Mrs Pearson dropped her voice to a whisper. 'I mean, do you think something's come through? Do you suppose whatever it is is in there now—deprocessing, or whathaveyou?'

'What? No. It's—I don't know.' Mr Pearson rummaged in his inside jacket pocket and brought out a fold of grey printed papers, typed up for him that afternoon using both black and red ribbons. He ran his finger down the list of instructions. 'Ah.' He tapped the pages. 'It's locked in.' He rechecked the relevant line. 'Yes. A red light means it's locked in. That's all.' He carried on reading. He nodded. 'Yes. It's automatic, see? They'll be doing something their end. And so at our end we do—nothing. Yes. For now we—we just wait.' He looked up again and smiled.

Mrs Pearson gave a small weary moan and walked away towards the sink. 'Well, I'm not wasting any more time hanging about. It's *your* work after all. It may not be your job, mind, but it's *your* responsibility. So it's likely you'll be the one to—' She took a large saucepan from the rack and began filling it with water. 'Are they paying you extra for this? You'd better be getting something. *We'd* better be getting something. For the inconvenience, I mean. Here for the whole weekend is what they said. What if we'd had guests? They never asked. And don't say they told you it'd be a privilege. If it's work it should be paid. And in any case what are the dangers? Being tested like lab rats, we are. Did they even try to provide any assurance it was all perfectly—'

Mrs Pearson dropped the heavy pan. It fell with a dull clatter back into the sink. The water jumped, slopping out over her apron and splashing to the floor.

Her hands had instinctively shot up to cover her ears. Yet the noise that made her do so had already stopped. All that could now be heard was the water running cold into the basin.

Mrs Pearson's mouth was fixed wide, ready to cry out. Her eyes were screwed small in further readiness for whatever might come next.

But nothing came next.

Turning about she saw how her husband too had both hands clapped firmly over his ears, his body bent double as he tightened into himself.

The noise hadn't lasted long, barely more than a second, having stopped as abruptly as it had started. For all its loudness it didn't actually hurt to hear it, but it was deeply unpleasant. Like the air was being scratched at with steel claws and torn apart, ripped suddenly open with the force of a hurricane and then just as forcefully snapped shut.

Mrs Pearson had an urge to vomit. She imagined her husband probably felt the same, though he'd never admit it. But in the new silence the sickening sensation quickly faded. Already Mr Pearson had straightened up and thrust his trembling hands back into his pockets. He gave his wife a brave and knowing look as if to say, *you see?* As if he had been wholly right in his predictions. But Mrs Pearson could still detect the grimace her husband was suppressing behind his tight-lipped smile as inwardly he shied from whatever new unpleasantness might follow.

Then the red light blinked off, its glow diminishing within the bulb, and, after the briefest of pauses, as though the machine were doing one final rapid check of itself before proceeding, the green light came on.

Mrs Pearson cautiously uncovered her ears. With a tentative hand she screwed the cold tap off, tight, before coming over to stand beside her husband.

'Do you suppose that means—' She stood with her shoulders a little hunched, drying her fingers on the corner of her apron.

Mr Pearson had resumed his easy stance, his muscles slowly relaxing, though his breath for the moment was stilled within his throat and all he could do by way of response was give a few short nods.

'So, how do we—' Mrs Pearson viewed the machine suspiciously. 'How will we even—know? For certain, I mean.'

Mr Pearson opened and shut his lips, fishlike, as he stared at the machine. Then he dug for his printed papers and consulted them closely. His hands were still trembling. He stepped forward. He glanced down once more, checking the instructions, before reaching up and grasping the top handle. It bent back easily on its hinge as he pulled it and, with a low soft clunk as the inner lock was released and the suck of plastic beading coming unstuck, the upper door opened and was allowed to swing freely outwards.

The compartment it revealed was a lot smaller than expected. The unit behind the door was mostly solid and of the same painted-grey as the rest of the machine, but with a hollow at its middle hardly big enough to house a box of eggs. This interior space was curved and its walls were lined with what looked like many tiny light bulbs, densely packed. They were of clear glass but with no visible filament, only a darkened centre, like a thousand fish eyes with large soft-edged pupils, or like a wall of hardened frogspawn.

A curved patch of these bulbs also centred the inside surface of the door so that when the unit was closed they would nestle into the hollow and complete the sphere. But for now that hollow was opened up. The bulbs lay dull and silent. And lying upon them, at their very middle, was a small white plastic spoon.

It looked to be of the same sort Mr Pearson encountered daily, when lunching at the institute canteen. He reached out to take it.

'Don't!' His wife smacked his outstretched hand away. 'It'll be hot, or electrified, or—something! *You* don't know.'

Mr Pearson consulted his notes carefully and shook his head. He reached into the compartment. He touched the spoon. It moved, squeaking lightly as it scraped against the delicate glass of the bulbs. Mr Pearson lifted it out. He looked at it in wonder. He showed it to his wife who bent her head in close to see that it was indeed a small white plastic spoon. Mr Pearson turned it over in his hands. He smoothed his thumb into its bowl. He felt along its edge for the rough seam of its moulded plastic. Then, carefully, deferentially, he placed it back into the glass-eyed hollow of the machine and began to shut the door.

'Won't they want to send something else through? Shouldn't we keep that one out in case they get, you know, muddled up?'

'No.' Mr Pearson spoke very gently, almost in a whisper. 'No, it's not like that. Not at all. Now we get to—' He eased the door closed, the glass bulbs creaking as they slid over each other to fit snugly in place. 'Now we send it back.'

He shuffled round to the side of the machine, his head bowed, his notes clutched tight in one hand, a stiff and purposeful finger pecking cautiously at the keypad.

'And you know just how to do that, yes? You're sure you actually know?'

Mr Pearson remained silent, focused on his task. His eyes flicked between the narrow display screen and his typed instructions. His lips moved noiselessly as he read the numbers back to himself, ensuring they matched. He hesitated, his finger above the button, ready to transmit. It was all just a little too easy, a little too straightforward. He smiled. Of course it was easy. The whole point was that it should be easy. That was the very reason they were giving him the opportunity to test such a device, from his own home, without supervision. He pressed the button and stepped back. The green lamp went out. The amber light came on.

At once a dreadful knocking began. A rapid internal hammering. Mr and Mrs Pearson looked at each other in alarm and then at the machine.

'Check your notes!' Mrs Pearson prodded her husband. 'See if that's normal, before this thing explodes and ruins our kitchen!'

The notes were duly checked. There was a frantic turning of pages.

The rattling and drumming noises continued, the different rhythms overlapping and warping, interfering with each other. There was a sound as of suction pumps, as of creaking pipes, a deep pulsing and surging.

'It says—it says that's normal.' Mr Pearson tried to appear relaxed, despite having to raise his voice above the racket. He forced a fresh smile to reassure his wife. 'It says we're to expect a slight audible disturbance. It's part of the whole, you know—the analysis procedure. It must be—yes, it needs to be thorough.'

'And how long would you say this thoroughness lasts exactly?'

Mrs Pearson was not in the least reassured. She had covered her ears again, but it made little difference, the sound seemed to get right inside her.

Taking small backward steps she retreated to the other side of the kitchen. Her husband followed suit, on the pretext of not wanting to shout, though when at length he opened his mouth to speak the knocking abruptly stopped. They both glanced at each other, then back at the unit. The amber bulb was still lit.

Mr Pearson put his hands to his ears also. There was the feeling that anything might now happen, and without clear warning.

But nothing did. The machine remained silent and still.

Mrs Pearson dared, tentatively, to uncover her ears.

'Well, I can tell you, I don't much feel like cooking any more. Not with that thing in here, about to go off who-knows-when. It wouldn't be safe, putting the hob on. Who'd ever want to live with such a thing? It's disconcerting, to say the least. It's ugly too.'

'It's only a prototype. I'm sure once they've sorted out the mechanics of the thing it won't sound anything like it does now. They'll fix that. They'll smooth it all out. And I'm not especially hungry anyway. A sandwich or some such will do me just fine.'

Mrs Pearson set to, preparing them both a simple cold supper, though she didn't like having to cross near the machine to get to the larder.

Mr Pearson sat himself at the table. In this apparent new calm his eagerness had returned.

'Bit of a marvel though, wouldn't you say? This'll be the start of a new era. This is the future, right here in our kitchen!'

'I don't really see what difference it'll make. Sending disposable spoons.'

'Oh, don't be daft. Spoons is only for testing. Simple things, see? One small item at a time while they make sure it's properly, you know—calibrated or whatnot. You need to think bigger than that. The machines they have at the institute are—well, I've not personally seen them, but I'll wager they're pretty enormous. And just you imagine a big foreign factory with whole ware-houses devoted to sending their goods out like this. You could have a new load sent every second. Just like that.' He snapped his fingers. 'Like lightning. Arriving at its destination in an instant. All ready for use.'

'Not likely.' Mrs Pearson glanced at the amber light. 'Not if you have to wait this long each time you send anything.' She set down two full plates and seated her-self at the table.

'They'll sort that out. It'll be instant. You mark my words.' Mr Pearson took a hunk of bread and began to butter it, waving his knife from time to time to conduct his thoughts more precisely. 'And not spoons. No. I'm thinking it'll be iron and steel and crude oil and such-like. Raw materials. Things it takes months to deliver from abroad with conventional shipping. Once they've put the cabling down, that is. Ocean floor stuff. That'll take a good while, no doubt. A lot of work involved in that sort of operation. But it'll be worth it. Far cheaper in the long run.'

'And it'll put all the regular companies out of business, too. All the ship-builders, the engineers, the able seamen. All out of work. In an instant. Like lightning. Not much of a future for them.'

'Not true. Not true at all.' Mr Pearson pointed the tip of his knife with intent, pausing the discourse as he chewed and swallowed a large mouthful. 'For one thing, they'll still be in service for all those other goods. All those items that can't be sent via the new method. Complicated goods, you know, like electrical devices, or luxury foodstuffs. Not to mention people themselves. They'll still need to get around. And secondly, even if the shipping industry does, as you quite rightly suggest it might, become defunct, well then, all those workers can join this new industry. Plenty of jobs there, I'd imagine. Monitoring systems. Laying more cables. That sort of thing. One door closes, another opens. That's the way of things. That's progress.'

The knocking began again behind them. Mrs Pearson tensed with the suddenness of it and very nearly choked. Her husband waved the disturbance away in the manner of an expert thoroughly accustomed to the machine's workings.

'Reanalysis. That's all. It'll do that at intervals. Things change, you see. On a molecular level. From moment to moment. It'll reassess the object and recheck its sums or whatnot, and then it'll be all up to date when it's ready at last to send, when they're all set to receive it their end.'

'And how about us?' Mrs Pearson took a careful sip of water. 'How are we expected to benefit from this fabulous invention? How is someone like you, in Personnel, going to profit from this new and improved world?'

'Why, as consumers, of course. It's not just about industry. We're the ones who benefit at the end of the day. Things will be cheaper. More convenient. One day spoons, another day whole cars. Maybe. Delivered straight from factory floor to our front door. Or to the front drive, rather. Or to the nearest place with one of these machines installed. That's got to be cheaper, and less bother, and all-round-better, wouldn't you say?'

'It all sounds that much more expensive if you ask me. Just more money being wasted. All rather unnecessary.' Mrs Pearson stood with her empty plate and glass and moved to the sink. 'All those many miles of wiring needing to be laid. All the new machinery. That's bound to bump the cost of goods *up*, not lower it.' She tilted her head. 'Or who knows, maybe on balance it'll all just stay the same. Pricewise, I mean. That's the usual way of things. Nothing ever really changes. Comparatively speaking.'

She didn't like the noise, the knocking and sucking and gurgling, but already she was able to ignore it; like having workmen digging up the road, right outside the house, one soon regarded it as mere background noise. But when the knocking from the machine stopped and she sensed that the light had changed, silently, serenely, from amber to red, her own demeanour rapidly shifted, and she placed her dishes quickly in the sink and clamped both hands over her ears and shut her eyes. Mr Pearson quickly followed her example, and they both stayed that way, stiff, awaiting the horrible ripping noise that, when it came, would surely make them want to throw back up what they'd just swallowed down.

It felt even worse than the first time. Even though they'd been expecting it. Even with their ears covered. They felt a sudden tug, brief but very strong. That same ripping, clawing noise now yanked at their insides. It dragged them fractionally in the direction of the machine.

Tentatively they opened their eyes. The light on top of the unit was green once again. Mr Pearson swayed from his seat, trying to move in a way that suggested he found movement easy. He went to check the chamber. It was entirely empty. Nothing to be seen but the tight array of glass bulbs. It was like a magic trick. No route in, no route out. Now you see it, now you don't.

'It's a big enough machine.' Mrs Pearson was pressing the flat of both hands to her belly. She didn't quite straighten to her full height as she came over to stand beside her husband, to peer with him into the empty chamber. 'There could be a hidden panel. Those bulbs could open like a trapdoor and down the spoon goes. Held just out of sight. Then close the door and *pop*, up it comes again.'

Mr Pearson reached in a hand and stroked the floor and walls of the chamber. The glass bumps of the bulbs seemed preternaturally smooth to his probing fingertips.

They were slippery and cool and he was surprised not to find his hand wet as he withdrew it.

'They seem pretty firmly set. Pretty tightly packed.'

'And that spoon was just a little thing. Look at the size of that cable. It's nothing special to get a spoon through there.' Mrs Pearson undid her apron strings and folded the stained white cotton neatly in her hands. 'Must be some sort of vacuum tube system. You know, pneumatics or suchlike. Like they have in them fancy banks. All that knocking, that's just building up the pressure, and then—*fwoop*—off it goes. Just like that. Very clever, I'm sure, but nothing new, and it won't catch on.'

Mr Pearson nodded slowly. He wasn't altogether listening. He was rocking the open door on its thick hinges. He was trying to get a sense of the weight of it. He was looking to see what fine wiring connected the door to the main unit.

Mrs Pearson left him to it.

'Well, I'm certainly not waiting for them to send more spoons.' She placed the folded apron on the table beside the remnants of their small supper. 'And I really hope they don't. Not tonight.' She glanced at the unwashed dishes in the sink. 'All that knocking and throbbing and screeching. I'll be lucky to get a wink of sleep.' She took a deep breath and headed for the hallway. 'Just mind that you pull the door to when you come up.' And she was gone.

Mr Pearson stood for a moment alone. The machine before him was silent. With his wife out of the room he could now appreciate just how utterly silent the machine was. Even a refrigerator would hum quietly, but this thing had no such background buzz, not even from the glowing green lamp. It made Mr Pearson's own nasal breathing sound coarse. The door as he swung it gently shut gave nothing back to his hand, no sense of friction in the hinges, not until the glass bulbs came in contact with one another, at which there was a brief moment of resistance and that fine high-pitched creak as they rubbed, before the magnetic strip around the door sucked itself shut to the frame with a small soft thud.

Mr Pearson put his hands in his pockets and walked backwards a few steps, not wanting to take his eyes off the machine, not just yet, in case something happened, something unusual.

But nothing happened. The green light remained lit. The machine remained silent. And soon Mr Pearson turned about and, slouching, followed his wife upstairs to bed.

¶

There was the cool blue dark of the kitchen and the soft yellow light from the streetlamp coming in through the cracks of the window's slatted blinds. There was the dull heavy presence of the machine standing ready and the small steady glow of its amber bulb above.

There was a sound of slow creaking. There was a gentle thumping, deep and soft and hesitant. There was a shuffling, a fumbling in the dimness, and the kitchen door, still ajar, swung slowly inwards.

The blurry shadowy shape of Mrs Pearson stood in the doorway, the thin yellow light faintly edging her worn white nightgown. She stood hugging herself. She reached out a bare foot and pressed her big toe against the thick length of cable that snaked in through the doorway. Its rubber was soft and warm. It gave a little under her touch.

She padded to the sink, her naked feet making small sticky noises on the cool linoleum floor. She crouched low, her knees together, opened the cupboard door and, reaching in under the sink, slid out a long canvas toolbag. She stood and the bag sagged at either end as the weight of metal it held shifted.

There were no sounds in the road outside. The whole street was asleep. But the machine with its amber light imposed its ever-readiness on the room. At the low wall socket behind it Mrs Pearson put her hand to the small brown plug. It felt hot. The wire too was hot. She switched off the current and watched as, a second or so later, the amber light on top of the unit faded into the kitchen's blueness. Mrs Pearson wriggled the plug from its socket, just to be certain, and laid it silently upon the floor.

Feeling around in the toolbag she found a long black rubber torch. She pointed it at her feet before turning it on. It was startling in its brightness and she put her splayed fingers over its end to filter the beam before shining it over the lower part of the machine, searching for screws. There were eight on the nearside panel and she rummaged again in the toolbag for the screwdriver that would fit them best, before angling the torch beam onto the machine's front edge and setting to work.

The screws were set flush to the metal. They were done up very tight. But Mrs Pearson was determined. She gritted her teeth till her jaw ached. She gripped the screwdriver so hard her knuckles whitened, and she twisted with all her might till with a small metallic creak the first screwhead was suddenly loosened. Gently she unwound it till it fell into her palm.

She had six screws out, neatly arranged on the floor beside her so she could be sure in what order to put them back, when she realised that her little shuffles and grunts of exertion weren't the only night noises in the kitchen. Another shadow was standing in the doorway, watching her. Glancing up from the small bright cone of torchlight Mrs Pearson's eyes took a moment to readjust before she could make out the pale stripes of her husband's pyjamas.

The two stood staring at each other for a while across the darkness. Then Mr Pearson came into the room. He was wearing old leather slippers and his tread fell very soft on the kitchen floor. He stood looking down at his wife. The torch beam spread its light over the scene, giving long sharp shadows to the neat arrangement of screws, showing the clear gap where the machine's side panel had part-sprung away from the body.

Mr Pearson held out his hand. Mrs Pearson put the screwdriver she'd been holding into his palm. Mr Pearson gripped it firmly then applied the screwdriver's tip to one of the last two upper screws, and began to twist. Mrs Pearson found another screwdriver for herself and joined her husband in the work.

They were very careful in not letting the panel fall when at length they'd got it free. Together they caught its sudden weight and together they rested it up against the kitchen wall. They shone the torch deep into the machine.

At first they couldn't be sure what they were seeing. The movement of the torch as its light shifted through the interior gave the sense that something in there was alive. It looked like a lot of bright red worms, all writhing over one another, seething in a great mass. Of course it was no more than wires. Thousands of fine red wires. There was not much else to be seen, just a narrow central column and several flat hanging panels, like vanes in a radiator, or like thin wooden frames in a beehive. Out of these panels flowed the wires, all of them overlapping and tangling, connecting this with that, and that with something else. It was like a hugely complicated switchboard. Shining the torch in closer they could see that each tiny connection point on the boards had a minuscule code, printed onto the metal in fine white type.

Mr Pearson pushed the head of the torch in deeper, angling the beam upwards. Just more switchboards. More wiring. He wondered if the number of wires related to the number of spawn-like bulbs there were in the upper hollow of the unit. Or perhaps it would be that number squared. Perhaps cubed. At a small cry from his wife he quickly withdrew the torch. He shone it on her hands.

She had pricked her fingertip. The mounting points for the wires were very sharp. One bright bead of blood was slowly blooming from her skin.

Hurriedly the two of them lifted the side panel up against the machine and screwed it firmly back in place. They wiped down all the surfaces they'd touched, first with a wrung-out dishcloth, then a tea towel. Lastly the small brown plug was put back in the wall socket.

They held their breath as they switched on the power. A few seconds later the amber light once again began to glow.

Mr and Mrs Pearson breathed out as one. Toolbag and torch were hastily hidden away.

Together the pair shuffled back upstairs to bed.

¶

Mr Pearson was out fetching the Saturday papers when men from the institute arrived the following morning to collect their prototype. They hardly spoke to Mrs Pearson other than in asking, politely, to be allowed in.

There seemed to be no special shut-down procedure. The wall socket was turned off, the wire was wound up, the cable was uncoupled, the machine was wheeled out and into the waiting van. The driver tipped his cap to Mrs Pearson and she watched them drive away.

Back in her kitchen she stared for a moment at the spot on which the machine had stood all through the night. There were four deep indentations, arranged in a tidy square, from where it had pressed its bulk into the lino.

From her pocket Mrs Pearson removed a short length of fine red wire. It was tipped at either end with sharp brass connectors. She examined it closely, turning it slowly between her fingers before laying it to one side on the kitchen table, as now she began to clear the breakfast things.

2. One Way

EMMA LEANED from the cab window as her colleague Krištof slow-steered their lorry down the wide quiet roads of the residential estate. Stefan, sitting between them, was supposed to be watching the opposite side of the road to Emma, but he was rolling cigarettes from a tin on his lap. The problem with any removals job was always the same, not in locating the house itself but in locating the nearest connection box to it.

Emma's recent phone call with the client had been unusually tiresome but she'd maintained her patience as the woman on the end of the line had left the phone hanging then shuffled on her coat and stepped out the front door to wander down the road in search of the sort of box Emma had described.

These boxes were painted a neutral grey and despite their size were easily ignorable, near invisible to all but the most astute of passers-by. Few would remember their installation, or what they had replaced. It was the sort of street object that had somehow always been present.

'There!' Emma pointed straight ahead through the windscreen. 'Between—well, behind those two brown cars. Looks like you can pull in alright just beyond them.'

Krištof neither increased his speed nor nodded in acknowledgement of the sighting. Perhaps he too had seen the box and had simply not said. Perhaps he resented Emma's eagerness, her efficiency, her need always to point out the obvious. The trip so far had been much like this: Emma trying her best to be engaging and the two men sitting beside her mostly mute, talking only when an answer was unavoidable, and only then with the simplest of phrasings.

Emma squinted hard at the numbers of the houses as they passed.

'Yes, this looks about right. She should be just around the next corner. Can probably get away with—just a single reel, wouldn't you say?'

She'd made her question deliberately direct but again there was no response from the two men. Perhaps they didn't like to speak without being certain. Perhaps they were silently calculating the distance as they drove. Emma pretended she hadn't wanted a response anyway. Putting her canteen to her lips she sat back and gazed out her open window.

It was a hot day. Hardly a breath of wind outside. Now that they'd slowed there was no longer any blow-through into the cab. The heat coming in from the windscreen was thick and oppressive. The houses they passed were all of the same style: small, red, detached, with perfectly flat, perfectly rectangular front lawns and narrow driveways bordered by low uneven walls of rough grey stone.

Ahead they saw someone sitting in the very centre of one of these lawns, alone, on a foldable garden-chair, her face hidden beneath a large pale floppy-brimmed hat. The figure stood as the vehicle approached. An elderly lady, tall but stooped, who, without signalling the lorry, turned now, folded up her chair, and carried it back into her house.

Krištof parked with the tail of the lorry as close in to the driveway as he could get it and Emma, leaving the two men to their duties, headed across the scorched yellow lawn to the front door. The lady was gone but the door was still wide open, with only the inner fly screen left across. Emma knocked on the glass of the nearest window.

'Mrs Carter?' Emma heard no answer from within, but she continued her introduction anyway. 'We're the removal firm you hired. I hope we've not arrived too early.' She didn't herself believe that being early qualified as an inconvenience but it was better to pre-empt any such criticism. 'Mrs—Carter?' There seemed to be movement in the darkness of the house, though no one was coming any further forward and Emma cupped her eyes to see better through the fly screen's mesh. 'It'll take a while for the chaps to set up, but if I could get a quick look at what you've got, at how you've arranged things, at doorways and suchlike, well then, that would—at least—Mrs Carter?'

The movement inside the house came closer. The fly screen was swung open and there the old lady stood, tall and gaunt, in a beige summer dress and worn white cardigan, her large brown eyes looking down at her visitor in a manner both dissatisfied and resigned. The sun-hat had been taken off, revealing wiry black hair pulled tight into a bun, and only very lightly streaked with grey.

'Emma.' Emma held out her hand, smiling broadly, determinedly.

The elderly lady allowed her own hand to be held and shaken but she did not return the grip and stared out beyond Emma to the lorry, to the two men unspooling a thick black cable along the pavement, stopping every few yards to kick it close in to the wall and dropping low wooden ramps over it where it spanned open driveways.

'No. I don't like it.' Mrs Carter gave a little shake of her head, as though this simple statement was the end of a long and tiresome discussion she'd been having with herself. She turned to walk back inside. 'What does it matter what I like though, hmm? What choice do I have?'

Emma didn't feel these questions were really for her but she wasn't going to pass up the opportunity for conversation. 'What choice do any of us have, Mrs Carter? Nobody likes moving house. I can't pretend to you that any of our clients have ever expressed enjoyment on the day.' She followed the old lady inside before the screen door began to swing shut again. 'But we do try to make things, well, fuss free. You know? Smooth. Easy-going. In effect we try to make your—'

The house was dark and cool. There were no carpets, nor even rugs to cover the highly-polished golden brown of the parquet flooring. Emma tried not to think what her colleagues' boots would do to that varnish as they traipsed in and out with heavy furniture. At least the old lady would be moving on before the day was through.

'Here.' Mrs Carter had stopped in the centre of an open hall from which the stairs curved up towards a narrow landing. 'Best if they start here.' She pointed to several stacked cardboard boxes. 'You'll see I've put tags on everything. Everything *with* a tag is to go. If there's *no* tag, it stays. You understand? Will your men understand? You mustn't let any unlabelled items leave this house. Not in your—contraption. Such items will be coming with me. Later.'

Emma glanced casually about her, taking in the scene, nodding. She had encountered this sort of behaviour on many occasions. She accepted it, even if she didn't entirely understand it. She'd learned early on there was little point in trying to persuade the client that there was nothing at all for them to worry about. Such people would never change their minds, even if practical evidence were provided.

'That's—very thoughtful of you, Mrs Carter. Makes our lives much easier.' She smiled and lifted the tag on the box nearest to her. It was blank. Just a paper label, its trailing thread taped crudely to the cardboard. 'I'll tell the boys. They'll appreciate that. You have no idea how many people don't give clear instructions. And then they go on and on at us if something isn't done exactly how they wanted, etc. etc.'

'Yes. Well. I believe it is important to be thorough.'

'It certainly is, Mrs C. It certainly is.' Emma patted the box.

It was a risk, abbreviating her name like that, but it seemed to pay off. The old lady's face softened a touch, and a small smile twitched momentarily on her lips.

'Quite. And you'll want to see the larger items, yes?' Mrs Carter turned around smartly and strode away into another room. 'The patio doors are unlocked, and the side gate round to the front can be pinned back, and if you do find you need—'

Emma smiled again, this time to herself, and followed at an easy pace. It looked like it was going to be a straightforward job after all. That is till Emma saw the baby grand piano and the antique chest of drawers and several other such cumbersome objects.

The smile dropped. It wasn't the size of these things that concerned Emma, that wasn't a problem at all, it was that not one of them had a brown tag attached.

¶

The rear doors of the lorry had been securely fastened back and the long battered ramp was down.

While Krištof and Stefan were in the house negotiating the larger items, explaining to Mrs Carter in short no-nonsense phrases that there really wasn't any option for their removal besides the one being offered, Emma climbed the ramp and unhooked her control unit on its extendable spiral cord.

She opened the secondary set of doors, just enough to step inside the main chamber; that springy length of flex being all she had to ensure the door could not be closed on her by accident. It was a simple but effective safety measure: if the cable was indeed severed by the door inexplicably closing then it would be impossible for the system to function.

The unlit chamber was cool and clean. Emma put the machine through the first of its checks, bringing a faint yellow glow to the ninety thousand or so small glass bulbs that lined the chamber's inner walls and roof. She glanced at a spot just above her. A bulb was out. The same bulb that was always out. It showed as a tiny black hole in the otherwise glowing honeycomb. She was through replacing it. It wouldn't make a difference anyhow. Theoretically up to two per cent of the bulbs could be failing with neither analysis nor transmission being compromised; at least so long as the faulty bulbs were uniformly scattered throughout the array, not all clustered into a single dark patch.

With no other black spots showing, Emma took a small carved soapstone figurine from the top pocket of her workshirt and placed it alone in the centre of the room before exiting the chamber herself and sealing the door. This simple test-analysis was fairly quick, the drumming and rattling and pulsing that came from inside the machine lasting barely a minute before the results came through on Emma's control panel. She scanned down the bright orange lines of data, clicking swiftly between the pages. She knew what patterns to expect. It was always easier to use a familiar test object, you tended to find exactly what you asked the machine to look for.

Emma retrieved her figurine just as Krištof and Stefan were bringing round the first items to be loaded. They'd got their way by simple dogged reasoning, convincing Mrs Carter that if she didn't allow them to transport all the big pieces of furniture then such items would never leave the house. No other option was available.

The piano came out first. Neither of the men was particularly large. Tall, yes, but not broad. Still, they carried the baby grand between them as though it was a mere toy, a folly made with hollow plastic keys and nylon strings, not something of lacquered maple and cast iron. In it went, to the very back of the chamber, and the two men at once headed off towards the house to fetch more.

'I was told it couldn't cope with things like pianos.' Mrs Carter was standing beside the ramp with her arms tightly folded and her pale sun-hat back on. She stared up at Emma from under the wide floppy brim. She spoke in a low voice. 'I read it somewhere. *Complex materials.* That's what the article said. Hardwoods. Felt. Ivory. It couldn't deal with them.'

'Used to be the case.' Emma nodded without looking round. 'Must have been an old article. Out of date.' She fiddled with the buttons on her control panel, trying to get a clear fix on the link-up. 'For early models, yes, anything organic was, as far as we know, a major problem. Not so these days. Much better depth-analysis. Just as long as it's not living matter, not actually animate, then—it's really no trouble.'

Krištof and Stefan continued to load item after item and Mrs Carter watched them without saying a word. Despite the heat neither man appeared to sweat. For them none of this seemed in the least bit strenuous, no matter the size and composition of the furniture being loaded.

'It doesn't seem right.' Mrs Carter fidgeted on the spot. 'All bunched up like that. All going in one go.'

Emma smiled to herself. 'Same as if we were to drive it. All bunched together. All done in a one-er.'

'And you still could drive it. You could simply load it up, in this very van, and drive it there yourselves.'

Emma paused. She stared up at the blue cloudless sky for a moment. 'Bit out of our way. And it might damage the equipment. Not to mention your belongings.

All that distance? On all those old roads? Potholes and the like? Broken glass? Accidents and hold-ups? For the insurance alone it'd be a great deal more expensive.'

'I was reading into that, too. The cost. It hasn't changed. No matter what they say. Not since my day. Not really. All this—' Mrs Carter waved a hand vaguely. 'New-fangledness. This rigmarole. And what difference does it actually make? How does it actually make things better? And for whom?'

'The price will come down, eventually. But you're sort of right. The service is essentially the same, so, to be frank, there's no real reason for the overall cost to change. Same service. More staff. Just a different, you know, outlay. A shift in what that money goes into.'

As Krištof closed the chamber door and bolted it, Mrs Carter unfolded her arms suddenly. 'That's not all of it. What are you doing? There's still plenty to—'

'It's okay, Mrs Carter. Be calm, be calm.' Emma hopped down from the ramp. Her tone was playful but the old lady didn't seem to notice. 'We do it in batches, that's all. Standard procedure. It gives the team at the other end a moment to unload it. And while they unload it *there* we load up the second lot *here*. Gets into a bit of a rhythm, see?' She pressed the go button.

The drumming and knocking and rattling began as before. Mrs Carter looked a little dazed.

'The other team? I—I hadn't thought.'

'Two lorries. Two teams. Senders and receivers. A direct connection, a link, between the two machines. You can hardly expect your furniture to appear just like that on the front lawn of your new house. And even if it could, well, who'd be around to carry it indoors?'

'Two teams. Yes. Of course.' Mrs Carter was staring into space. She seemed to be debating the matter with herself, her voice little more than a murmur. 'Indeed. Small wonder it costs so much. Two of everything, one must suppose. All so—complicated.'

The knocking from the lorry stopped. Mrs Carter glanced up sharply, expecting something to happen. Then she looked at Emma.

'Is that—that? Is it gone?'

Emma shook her head. 'Not yet. Need to wait for a window. Could take up to, say—five minutes? Maybe more. Depending on traffic.'

'The traffic? Are they not there yet?'

'The connection. A firm link-up. The network is pretty busy most days. Specially days like today. But once we get that good connection, once we're locked in—'

Emma's voice trailed off. She was looking at the display on her control panel. She was scrolling through the lists of data from the preliminary analysis.

Mrs Carter peered down at the screen also, but all she saw there was a lot of gobbledegook. She recognised the same sets of letters, even some of the words, but the phrase constructions made her feel as though she'd suddenly lost her faculty for language.

Emma glanced up. 'Sorry, Mrs Carter. This is the boring bit. Necessary, but boring. So I really do need to concentrate. And what with it being such a hot day and all.'

Mrs Carter stepped back. Her eyes were wide and she looked as though she might speak again, but she simply turned about and headed indoors.

Emma shaded the screen, putting her back to the sun and bending forward over the unit. This really was the important part, this was why she was here at all, the aspect of the job she was especially good at, aside from dealing with clients. She was looking for anomalies in the data stream. The feed coming through from the analysis really was gobbledegook, for the most part. It was machine-speak. That is, it wasn't really something anyone actually spoke, but Emma understood it, it's what she was trained for, and she could tell instantly when something didn't look right. It was like hearing a wrong note at a piano recital: it didn't matter how complicated the piece was or if you'd never heard it played before, so long as you had a good ear for music, and so long as you listened attentively, you simply knew, at once, that that single note should not be there among the rest.

But a mistake in a concert was one thing. Mistakes like that happened and nobody minded. Here such mistakes could not go so easily ignored.

Emma worked quickly but thoroughly. Not one line of code was overlooked, and when at length the light on her panel flashed to tell her they had a clear connection, she was satisfied, and without a second thought she pressed send.

The world jolted, briefly. A small sphere of birds burst from a tree and thrummed away into the hot blue sky. A brindled cat dashed across the road from under a parked car and disappeared into the garden opposite.

It was the usual sort of thing.

Emma remained very still, tensed at the edge of the ramp, her head bowed, her eyes screwed shut.

If there had been a dog barking a moment earlier, it wasn't barking now. If there had been grasshoppers scratching their insistent pulse out on the lawn they too had ceased. Emma could hear no distant wash of traffic from the motorway, but maybe it hadn't been there beforehand. She couldn't say for sure. The sudden silence had pressed everything flat.

When Emma opened her eyes the hard sunlight seemed thinner. The heat of the air was sharper. The quick gust that had risen in the breeze had settled abruptly into new and definitive calm.

Emma checked the display on her remote control. Then she hung it back on its hook and went into the house.

¶

The lounge, having been stripped of most of its fittings and furniture, did not feel like a place one could relax in any more. In the centre of the room, around a tall cardboard box, three simple bentwood chairs had been set. It looked like a small gathering for a game of cards around a makeshift table, or vagrants crowding close to a burning brazier. Except on top of the cardboard box was a painted wooden tray, which in turn supported a set of tea things: a pot with a woven bamboo handle, four small cups on deep-set saucers, a matching milk jug, a sugar-bowl with silver spoon protruding, and a small plate of shortbread fingers.

Emma wondered if the tea set had been unpacked specially. Krištof and Stefan were back at work in the end room, hauling the remaining items out the patio doors and round the side of the house. Only Mrs Carter sat beside the box, her knees neatly together, back arched and head dipped slightly forward, gazing wide-eyed at a spot on the skirting board. When Emma entered and took one of the seats, the old lady straightened, smiled, and began pouring a fresh cup.

'These came out of Shanghai with my family when we were forced, and I do mean *forced*, to return to this country. Carried in our luggage all this way. By boat, no less. They're extremely precious to me.'

The cups were of fine bone china, duck-egg blue, with paler dimples, small lozenge-shaped spots, patterning their sides.

'We always called them rice bowls. They're not for rice. Not these. It's the pattern, like rice, especially if you hold them up to the light. The dimples are very thin, very delicate. The light shines through them.'

The tea Mrs Carter poured was pale and yellowish. As its level rose inside the cup Emma saw the dimples turn to a faint green. Milk and sugar were added without question, but only a drop of milk and barely a few granules of brown sugar; hardly anything at all; hardly worth it. The milk flowered downwards through the yellow tea. The dark crystals of sugar punctured this inner pluming as they fell. A brief melodious stirring with the silver spoon, and the cup and saucer were lifted and presented to Emma.

'Part of a much larger set, you understand. And no, they won't be going via your—your *system*. They will travel with me.'

Emma said nothing. She sipped from the cup. It was good tea. She couldn't place the variety. But it was good.

'You see, it's the altogether unique items that have been worrying me. I'm old. Oh yes, you don't need to make a face. I've lived for longer than most. Unexpectedly so. I've collected a lot in my time. A lot has been passed on to me. Been put in my care, so to speak. And I couldn't bear it. You see? I just can't take such a risk.'

Emma thought she should perhaps nod sympathetically at this point, but for now she stayed as she was, just watching, letting Mrs Carter speak, allowing her to say whatever she felt she must.

'And my first thought, of course, was the jewellery. Yes. One tends to consider that first. And not simply for its value. Each piece has its story, has its personal connection. But, all in all, they don't take up much room. A simple zip-up leather case. An enamelled box.'

Emma smiled. This was something she was more familiar with. 'People always do that. It's a funny thing. But they always do it.' She set down her saucer and cup. 'Oh, it's okay. Don't worry. I do get it. I understand completely. But it's funny all the same.'

Mrs Carter eyed the girl quizzically.

'Because—don't you see? It's all just gold and silver and gemstones!' Emma smiled again. 'It's elements and compounds. Regular minerals. They may be precious but they are, in effect, the simplest of all materials. They each have a very uniform, a very well-defined, crystalline structure. They show up really beautifully on the analysis. You can always spot them. Very clear, very hard points of data.'

'For their materials, perhaps. They may be simple in that respect. But your machine can't so easily account for the artistry that went into making them, it can't capture the personal design, the skilled fashioning, the hammering, the heat, the very history of them.'

'Oh, but that's all just positional!' Emma laughed. 'That's what the machine's best at. Position and direction and speed and relative force. Right down to the subatomic level. It's quite incredible really. And very *very* accurate.'

Mrs Carter did not look at all impressed by this.

'But books, for example.' Emma put her head on one side. 'Now, that's a different matter. Books are essentially, well, blocks of wood.' She tapped the cardboard box with the toe of her shoe. The tea set it supported chimed and rattled in response. 'Fill a box like this with books and you've made yourself one big box-sized block of wood. Very heavy. Complicated too. All those fragile pages. Sliced and printed. And I've sometimes wondered—' Emma leaned forward and took one of the shortbread fingers. She dunked it in her tea thoughtfully. 'Say, what if a book was to arrive at the other end with all its words muddled. Still all the same letters, just rearranged. Would it be, in essence, the same book? So long as the information itself is retained, I mean. The same amount of ink, paper, board, cloth, but—you know, reordered. Or else all those words bunched up. A tight black hole in the centre of each page. The story would still be in there, somewhere. The sense of it might still come out, at some point. A sort of rare emission. Unlikely perhaps. But possible.'

Mrs Carter sat with a look of horror.

'I'm teasing, Mrs C.' Emma laughed again. 'That's not how these things work. That could never happen. Never ever! The machine just doesn't think like that.'

35

She downed the last of her tea and rose to her feet. 'In fact, the machine doesn't really think at all. That's the beauty of it!'

Krištof was standing beside them now. He was looking down at the box that supported the tea tray, a paper label protruding from its top edge. Mrs Carter tugged at the label till with a small ripping noise it came unstuck. She scrumpled it into her palm at once.

Krištof shrugged and headed back out. Emma followed at an easy pace.

¶

Outside it seemed now that regular noise had returned to the neighbourhood. Emma stood for a moment, listening, taking time to notice things this time round.

It wasn't particularly special. There was indeed a dog barking somewhere down the street. There was the sound of small birds chittering. There were insects in the grass. There was distant traffic noise. It was all very normal, though Emma considered how it being there now was in no way evidence of it having been there previously, with what continues not being a reliable proof for what has passed. Though if there had indeed been a change, then how quickly the animals returned, how quickly they accepted the disruption.

At the lorry the last of the items had been loaded. Stefan was closing the inner door as Emma mounted the ramp and reached forward to pick up her controller. She glanced through the gap into the compartment just before it was sealed and her body stiffened. She almost cried out for Stefan to stop.

She had seen a face. In among the boxes and crowded items of furniture, there had been a human face, still and serious, staring sternly back out at her. But in that same fraction of a second in which she noticed it Emma also understood it for what it really was: a large portrait. Nothing more. Just an old oil painting, its heavy ornate frame propped against the rest of the items. Not flesh, but linseed and pigment, taut cloth, wood and gilt.

How curious that in all the many jobs she'd done with the removals firm Emma had never once experienced such a sight. But she was glad too that she had at least noticed, that her reactions and her attention to detail were as heightened as she required them to be. She smiled. It would certainly be a nice shock for the receiving team when the transfer was complete and they opened the doors their end to find that same face staring angrily out at them.

Emma locked the system and ran the analysis. The usual noises started up from within, like a giant washing machine turning over, grinding and rolling and tumbling its heavy load.

Emma glanced down the street to where Krištof and Stefan were perched on a low brick wall, smoking and chatting, the blue-grey streams of smoke drifting on the hot air, dispersing their fine particles into invisibility.

The analysis stopped with a loud inelegant clunk, as though after all that tumbling the contents of the lorry had at length settled into a singular comfortable heap. Emma began looking through the pages of code.

Despite her practised speed and almost lazily scanning eyes, the anomaly was glaring when she saw it. She'd only ever seen such things in her initial training, and those were merely simulations, unreal. But this was as obvious as a whole wall of checkerboard with just a single square the wrong colour. Her eyes fixed on it at once. It was no more than numbers and letters, just like the rest of the code, but still it was like a gaping hole in an otherwise perfect net, or a ladder in a stocking, or a scar. It made no sense. It had no purpose being there.

Emma went to unlock the chamber door, but stopped herself. She was curious. The machine itself was ready to send. The machine itself didn't think anything was wrong. The machine itself didn't think at all. Only Emma had noticed the error, if error it could be called. What might happen if she gave the all-clear to send? What might come out the other end? She drew back her hand and looked at her controller—then pressed the button to run the analysis over again.

She glanced down the side of the lorry. Her colleagues hadn't moved. They either hadn't noticed that the machine was going through its motions once more or they simply didn't care. It made little difference to them either way; their work was to load or unload, what happened in between was not their preserve.

No heavy clunk this time when the analysis stopped. Its noises had in fact been altogether smoother, more regular. The ear played tricks, of course. There were so many overlapping sounds, phasing in and out with each other, nothing ever sounded the same twice. Emma checked the readout. It was different. The order was different. The same information but less random in its layout, as though the machine had this time understood its contents better, as though it had refined that initial scan. But that was not how it worked. The machine did not understand. It did not learn. Every instance was new and unique. Every instance was in itself the only instance.

There was no anomaly this time round. Emma gave the pages a second readthrough, but it was all as clear as it could be. There were no errors. The analysis was perfect. And the red diode on the controller was lit. They had a clear connection window. They were all set to go. Emma took a breath and held it. She pressed send.

That sudden silence again.

It was like she had momentarily blacked out, her senses re-emerging separately, with hearing the last to catch up. Emma unscrunched her eyes. Mrs Carter was striding out urgently over the lawn, her long thin arms waving above her head, her mouth making mute shapes, as if she was trying with great effort to speak but without her voicebox connected.

Then the noises of the world swam gently back.

'—on't send, don't send! You mustn't! My grandfather!' Mrs Carter was on the ramp of the lorry. She wobbled up past a slightly dazed Emma, who merely stared at her. 'My painting, it—it must be in there! You mustn't let it go!'

She had her hand on the chamber door. Its lock un-coupled smoothly, easily. There was a brief suck of air as she pulled the big door open and it swung back on perfectly balanced hinges. But the chamber itself was empty. All was gone. Mrs Carter stood staring at this new nothingness.

'It's alright, Mrs C. There's nothing to worry about. Look.' Emma stood up beside her, showing her the screen of the controller. 'The transfer was good. All's fine the other end. There's been no problem. Now they just need to unload, and then—that's that.'

'But how would they know? How could they possibly know anything?' Mrs Carter didn't look at the screen. She attempted to take a step forward, into the chamber, but drew her foot back sharply.

'It's very simple, actually, and not really about knowing. Not as such.' Emma tried to show her the screen again. 'You see, the receiving machine shows a full analysis too, as standard, and that gets sent back to my unit, automatically, and if it matches with our own report then we can be sure, we can be certain, that—'

'Oh, forget your blasted machine, and all your blasted analyses, and data sets, and link-ups! You just don't understand.' Mrs Carter turned about and clumped back down the ramp. 'You'll never understand. That painting was unique. Unique!'

Emma shrugged. 'Everything's unique, Mrs Carter. That's the way of all things.'

Mrs Carter ignored this, turning again on her heel and pointedly raising a finger. 'How can you accept that a work of art, something made with care and understanding and human hands, something applied in minute increments, layer upon layer, something both made of paint yet beyond the paint it's made of, something that abstracts the mere matter of its materials into something transcendent, beautiful, eternal—how can that being taken apart atom by atom and reassembled hundreds of miles away in an instant, how can that ever be the same as the original? It becomes no more than a fake, a mere copy, a false representation *of* that original.'

'Not a copy. No. That's not how it works.' Emma frowned and squinted down at the bulky control unit still clutched in her hands. 'The replication is perfect, you see. You said it yourself. Atom by atom. It isn't a copy at all. It's the real thing. Just—transported.'

'No.' Mrs Carter shook her head sorrowfully. 'No. It'll be a replica now. Nothing more. It's been devalued. Lost its true perfection. Its true perfection being that it was made imperfect, through uncertainty, through a mess of colour and visible brushstrokes into something that made sense of those—chaotic applications.'

'I'm sure you'll be fine with it once you see it.'

'Oh, it won't be him. It won't be that same face looking out at me.' She turned about, dejected. 'I'll know. I'll feel it. And the less I can prove it, the worse it'll be.' She began to walk back towards the house. 'He'll be a fraud on my wall. Nothing more than that. An impostor.'

Krištof and Stefan were already rolling the cable back on its reel towards the lorry. Emma watched them for a moment as they packed everything away, both men ignorant of what had just happened. Though, in truth, nothing had happened. Nothing out of the ordinary. After a while Emma took the paperwork into the house for Mrs Carter to sign.

The old lady was shifting a few small boxes down from upstairs. There seemed to be quite a lot still left to remove. She signed the papers in silence.

'Are you sure you can manage all this, Mrs Carter?'

'Yes.'

'We could easily do another quick batch.'

'No, thank you.'

'We wouldn't charge extra.'

'It's quite alright.'

'It'll annoy the boys but they'll do it. I only have to tell them.'

'Please, just go now. You've already done enough.'

Emma took a single step back. She paused, then left, listening to Mrs Carter's mutterings fading away behind her.

'—should've been done the old way. Nothing wrong with the old way. Good hard work. Simple. Done for hundreds of years. Thousands. Never a problem—'

The lorry was all packed up and secured. Emma clambered into the cab. Krištof was looking out his window at the old woman: struggling as she carted boxes to the old estate car that poked its rear end from the garage.

'It won't get all in in one go.' Krištof tipped his head to one side. 'Three trips, I say she'll need. It will take her a long long while.'

Stefan leaned forward to look past his colleague. 'She'll do herself injury. Shouldn't carry that way. Not good distribution of weight. Centre of balance is off. Is all wrong.'

'Might get more damage in transit.' Krištof started the lorry. It grumbled then lurched forward gently as they moved off from the kerb. 'Then again—maybe not.'

'She might be having accident during trip. Might break herself.' Stefan sat back. 'Or—perhaps not.'

'Yes. Always possible something goes wrong.'

'Yes. That is always the way of things.'

3. First, Man

A NEW day was dawning and Frank was the first man to feel it. The forest behind his house was slowly waking, with rising mist and soft thin light and the noise of little birds, and he was the first man to pass through it.

The forest's red floor was spongy from the long fall of pine needles, a slow accumulation through the years, but it was the steady soft pounding of Frank's feet that the floor now supported. The tips of sunken stones and the ridges of slow-searching tree roots disrupted the clean line of the path, but Frank's running shoes trod firmly upon them, finding their angles, their roughnesses, a momentary grip and release as he pushed on up the slope.

Frank's breathing was not laboured. There was no ache in his muscles, only the glow of warmth as they worked to his will. His footfalls beat the ground quietly, with unflagging regularity. He saw a young deer step out of the trees and onto the path ahead of him, its shape solidifying through the misty light as he closed in upon it. The deer was dreamy in its calm, in its lightly stepping unhurriedness. Its ears flicked. It heard the approach. It lifted and turned its narrow head, considering the keen determination of the runner's movements.

The deer bolted. A sudden springing away, soon settling to a more controlled gangle-legged trot up the path. But Frank kept on close behind it, watching how it picked out its steps upon the path no better than he did, watching fear and confusion ripple through its muscles as it zig-zagged indecisively from one edge of the path to the other, its head held high, its ears back, till it found a suitable gap in the dense pine trees and darted away between them and out of sight. And Frank passed the same gap without looking, without slowing, continuing on through the forest. He would permit no distractions.

Scrambling up a steep bank Frank's feet tore at a matting of moss, uprooting it from its weak hold upon the soil to roll away behind him, but he barely broke step to correct the slip. Mushrooms grew in wide fairy rings, only to be crushed as he ran on through them, their rubbery mulch imprinted with his sole. Nothing could stop him and nothing would. He was superior to all. He was perfection. He was indeed the culmination of all life. Even mountains were no obstacle for him. He vaulted up their sides. He stood upon their peaks. He gazed down into the depths of the valley, his hands on his hips. He breathed fully and surely. His eyes were bright. His skin was hot.

He paused, and the world paused too. It awaited his next move. It waited for him to step back out from that high position, to begin the long downward run.

¶

Kathy was up and dressed and sitting at the kitchen table when Frank arrived home. She heard his slow deep breathing as he leant against the jamb of the open back door, prising off his damp running shoes, hanging them on their allotted peg, straightening their long wet laces into neat even lines to point at the red tiles below.

Kathy sat bowed over the table, her back to the door, one hand round a cup of coffee, the other flicking idly through one of her monthly magazines.

'Is it ready?' Frank could smell the cooked breakfast easily enough though there was no sign of it.

Kathy nodded without looking round.

'In the oven?'

'Mm-hm.' Kathy turned another page without reading any of what was on it. 'Just keeping warm. Foil on. It'll be ready when you want it. How was your jog? See anything nice?'

Frank didn't answer but stood for a moment, tensing his jaw as he stared at the back of his wife's head, its untidy knot of dark hair held up with a thin red rag. Then he turned and sprang lightly up the narrow steep staircase to the bathroom.

As he stripped he looked at himself in the mirror, at the gradual revealing of his body with each item of clothing he peeled away. His torso was glossy and smooth and damp and beautiful. He felt no shame in finding his own body beautiful. He worked hard every day to keep it in peak condition. He delighted in seeing it at its best. And it always looked best at this moment, just after his morning run, the fine curves of his muscles pushing out against the tightness of his skin.

Frank slipped his pants down to his ankles. Affixed to his right buttock was a small bandage pad: a thick white square of folded gauze held on with a cross of yellowing surgical tape. He tried to peel it back, teasing at one of the tape's torn edges, but it was still stuck fast to his skin.

He pushed a finger tentatively under the gauze. There was no pain, not any more. Not even tenderness. He stepped into the bath tub and drew the curtain halfway. Turning the taps to their precise positions he ducked straight under the cool spray from the showerhead with his eyes shut, breathing through clenched teeth as the temperature rose.

Kathy came in.

Frank heard her. He didn't open his eyes but stood statuelike under the hot spray, letting the water run through his short-cropped hair and down his body. Kathy eyed him for a moment before easing up her skirt and seating herself on the toilet beside the bath.

'I've told you before. I don't want you peeing while I shower.' Frank still hadn't opened his eyes. He hadn't moved. Hearing the creak of the lid being raised and the shuffle of his wife seating herself was enough. 'With all this steam. It'll lift. It'll mix in the air. It's unhygienic.'

'Then they shouldn't have built the bowl next to the bath.'

'The position dictates appropriate usage.' Frank began soaping himself. 'It's not hard to wait. Or to pre-empt.'

'If I need to go, I'll go. And, until we get another fitted downstairs, I'll go right here. You know we could afford an extension, easily. Convert that old tool shed you never use. Or would you prefer I wet myself.'

'Don't be so foul. You could always go outside. You know you could. No one's there to see you. No one but magpies and foxes.'

'Thanks. Now I can't go.' Kathy bowed forward, her brow almost touching her knees. 'Not right away.' She turned her head a touch to look at him. He was not a large man. 'All that exercise and you never seem to grow any bigger.'

'It's not about size, it's all a matter of—'

'Fitness.' Kathy squeezed her eyes shut for a moment. 'Yes, I know.'

Frank's bandage pad was now thoroughly wet. He picked at it. He tugged gently at its soddenness, soaping the edges of the tape bit by bit, letting it pull at his skin as it came away: a fine glossy line of scar tissue slowly revealing itself beneath.

'What did they take this time?' Kathy, wincing one eye open, eyed the scar. 'What little bit of you have they added to their collection?'

'This time?' Frank touched his fingers to the mark. There were others just like it at points around his body. On his abdomen, or high on his chest, or over the dimples of his spine. Each scar small and discreet. Hardly noticeable. Little keyholes into his interior, now sealed up. 'No. They did this one a while back. Nothing more than a little flesh and fat.'

'I thought they had all that. I thought they'd already taken what—'

'They have. They had. They wanted to try it again. They wanted to see if the results would be any different. You know, second time around.'

'And so they'll try the same with your liver? Your heart? More tiny snippets of you? Little off-cuts to send through their ridiculous machine?'

'It's necessary.' Frank ignored the bitterness of his wife's tone. 'They need to be sure it's still me coming out the other side.'

'Small dead pieces of you, you mean.'

'Barely dead. It gets sent through fresh. That's very important. That's vital.'

'Sounds too much like the goldfish again to me, drowning in its water bowl. Sounds like that poor gecko losing its grip. What'll be lost of you when you go through, huh? What will come out wrong?'

'Where on earth do you pick up such idiotic tales?'

'You. You told me yourself. Don't you even remember?'

Frank laughed. 'Those things are all made up. They're scare stories. Just institute humour.'

'They sounded real to me. Specific. Not something one of your scientist chaps would invent.'

'Oh, these *chaps* have pretty wild imaginations. You'd be surprised.'

Frank turned off the shower. The last of the water gurgled down the plug hole. Kathy stood up and flushed.

'Anyhow, their recent method is much more effective.' Frank began drying himself. 'They've been using fresh ejaculate. So much easier to obtain. Much easier to analyse too. For consistency, I mean. And, unlike other tissues, it stays alive that much longer. Full of nutrients, see? Sort of self-sustaining.'

Kathy lowered her gaze. 'They use—what?'

Frank laughed again. 'Little pieces of me. Just like you said. Me in miniature. It's only sensible. Practical.' He rubbed gently at another small scar, this one on the side of his neck. 'A pity they didn't think of it sooner.' The old incision still tingled at his touch. 'But no matter. No harm done.'

'You never told me any of this. How do they—' Kathy leant back against the damp tiles. '—get it out of you?'

'They have their methods.' Frank bent forward to dry his feet, poking a corner of towel between his toes. 'It's clinical. It's efficient. Clean. I really don't have to do anything at all.'

'You mean you'll do it for them but you can't manage it for me.'

'What did you say?' Frank straightened. He stood very still, considering her, his jaw tensing and untensing.

'I just mean that when you're with me you never seem—' Kathy glanced out the bathroom window towards the forest. 'But with them, with your institute buddies, well, then it's no problem. A regular stream offered up, I imagine. On tap. No doubt you find them far more—'

Frank's movement was quick and precise. His arm flicked forward and his hand gripped Kathy's wrist and held it firmly. She struggled instinctively but there was little hope of pulling free. Frank yanked her towards him, then half-dragged her out of the bathroom and across the landing towards their bedroom.

'No!' Kathy dug her heels into the carpet, still trying to wrench away from her husband's unrelenting grip. 'Not now! Please! I'm sorry!' She put every ounce of her weight into tugging backwards but all she succeeded in doing was hurting herself, her joints and muscles merely pulling against each other. 'I was just teasing. I didn't mean it. Please. I don't want to.'

'Doesn't matter now.' Frank spoke softly through half-gritted teeth. He pushed Kathy onto the bed, one hand behind her head, bending her forward, pressing her face to the mattress. 'Doesn't matter what you do or don't want.' He raised her skirt and yanked her underwear down past her knees. He gripped her firmly round the waist. 'This is a man's right over his wife. This is *my* right.'

And Kathy very soon gave up struggling.

She knew if she couldn't stop him in that first instant it was hopeless to keep trying. If she fought back any further it wouldn't merely be pushing and tugging he'd use to get her to stay still. Resisting just made it hurt more. She buried her face in the rucked-up bedsheets. She closed her eyes.

'I'm sorry. I'm sorry.' And her body gave up too. She hated that part most of all, how she had no real control over her own physicality, how her body betrayed her, how the betrayal itself brought relief. 'I didn't know. I didn't mean anything by it.'

'*My right. A man's right.*' Frank's voice came out in hoarse broken whispers. He breathed heavily, with regular deep intakes of breath, timed between his sudden forceful thrusts. Precision was important. Control and focus were his priorities. He wasn't interested in Kathy's protestations. His own words helped him concentrate. They became a mantra in his mouth. '*A man's wife. His right. You made your vows. You agreed to this.*' Though he wasn't talking to her. His muttering was for him alone. As though in self-argument. Trying to convince himself. Succeeding. '*You wanted this. You knew this.*'

And Kathy lay quiet. She said nothing. Took no part in the argument. It was not for her to take part in. She stopped whimpering. She stopped squirming. She lay waiting, as each sudden heave from him juddered through her, pushing her face into the cotton topsheet that now no longer felt soft against her cheek. Till

50

Frank's efforts subsided and he half-withdrew half-fell from her and slumped down on the bed.

After a while Kathy rolled awkwardly onto her side. She watched Frank, his comfortable exhaustion beside her, his chest rising high and falling flat in long slow breaths, consistently, perfectly. Kathy reached down a tentative hand and felt between her legs. Nothing there but her own dampness, cooling. No sense of any discharge. Not from him.

She scanned his full length, examining his shape. She preferred him like this. Limp. Unintimidating. Tender, even.

He used to kiss her. Long ago. He used to notice her, how she looked, what she wore, if her hair had been cut or styled even slightly differently. He would know how she was feeling from her movements, her posture, her tone of voice. He would analyse every detail of her. As much attention given to her as to himself. Perhaps more even to her. He used to make her feel crazy with desire, just from that looking, from that careful scrutiny. He made her feel desirable.

'This thing they do to you.' Kathy reached out a hand to touch him, but drew back, letting her arm fall slack to the sheets. 'This clean clinical thing they do with such accuracy, such efficiency. Could they—could it be done here? Could it be done when you're inside me?'

Frank twisted his head to look at her. He squinted, flicking his gaze between her eyes, trying to ascertain her seriousness, whether or not she was really proposing such a measure.

'I mean we could easily afford it. A child, I mean.' Kathy glanced away from what she suspected was her husband's look of disgust. 'With what they're paying you. With this house. Right here. It'd want for nothing. Our child. We'd bring it up right.'

'And we will.' Frank sat up stiffly, still squinting, but not at Kathy. 'Eventually. And we'll do it our way. We don't need any interference.'

'But now. Why not now? Before you go through. In case something, you know—' Kathy swallowed. She tried meeting his glance again. 'Because if anything were to go wrong—'

Frank sighed and let himself flop back down onto the bed.

'Listen, Kathy. Nothing is going to go wrong. What do you think all these tests have been for? All this surety. Nothing will happen in any other way than the way they expect it to happen. They wouldn't go ahead otherwise. They just wouldn't.'

And with that word, that *listen*, Kathy knew there was still uncertainty in her husband's mind, there was still hesitation, perhaps even fear. Anyone who began a line so forcefully with words like *listen* or *look* or *now see here* had, in her opinion, already lost the argument and didn't believe in what they were saying, trying to cover their own misgivings by belittling whoever it was they were trying to convince.

'Besides, I really can't allow myself the distraction of a child. Or a pregnant wife, for that matter. I need to maintain peak—'

'Yes, yes, I know. Peak condition. In body and in mind. No extra worries. No unnecessary stress.'

Kathy leaned forward from the bed and stood up. But her husband was quicker. As though sensing her intent he rose smartly and pushed past her, then on into the bathroom.

The door was swiftly closed. Kathy heard the clack of the lock as the bolt was slid across. A moment later there came the sound of the shower being turned on once more.

Kathy eased her underwear back up and straightened her skirts, then headed on down to the kitchen.

¶

By the time Frank made his next appearance, in a grey shirt with matching woollen tie and carrying an old leather suitcase, his breakfast was ready and waiting, laid out on a pale green plate. A breakfast of bacon and black pudding, of fried egg and mushrooms, all carefully dabbed with a paper towel to remove any ooze of hot oil.

Kathy sat opposite while Frank ate, watching him. His head was down, his body angled stiffly forward over the table. She watched his careful dissection, the small slices from each separate foodstuff, picked out in a predetermined order, layered up onto his fork. She watched him pause now and again to take several quick sips from his mug of coffee, still holding to that forward inclination, not once looking up till his breakfast was finished, till the plate was as clean as he could make it, with only a few faint smears of misty grease congealing on the green.

Then the plate was pushed a handspan away from him, and the mug of coffee was drained of its last half inch and set back down.

'I was wondering.' Kathy gazed at him, her chin to her knuckles, her voice vague, dreamlike. 'Of all those little pieces they took from you. Did they ever take a biopsy of your brain?'

Frank held her gaze for a moment. Then slowly he leaned forward over the table. Kathy chose not to move, waiting as his face drew closer to hers.

It was strange, she saw the movement of his hand as it swung up, but she made no immediate effort to avoid it. It was something about his expression, about how she hadn't seen any clear sign of intent. She didn't quite believe he'd go through with the gesture, despite the speed of his swing. And so, when she felt the sudden smack of his palm across her cheek, and as she half-reeled from the shock of the blow, twisting herself away from the force of it, with her hair thrown into quick chaos as though from a sharp gust of wind, all she could think of was how it didn't hurt. Not in the moment of being struck. The pain, in that instant, was absent, deferred. Only the surprise of it was there: her own surprise at not having registered properly what was about to happen. And this was followed by a sort of fluster, a sort of panic, all coming too late, when she felt she should react, but didn't know how, and felt she should get out of the way, but didn't know where to. And then, of course, she felt the hotness of the sting spread through her skin, and the ache that was pulling at her jaw, but still she just sat there, stiff with that same surprise, one hand raised to her open mouth, as though to catch the sound, the familiar cry, that never came.

Frank leant slowly back in his chair. 'Look, I don't see why you're being so contrary.' He let his forearms lie flat to the top of the table either side of his empty plate. 'There's nothing about this they've not already thought out.' He stared at Kathy. She hadn't yet moved. Her hand still covering her mouth. Her eyes still fixed on her husband's. 'Somebody's got to be the first. That's just how it is.' Frank glanced away slightly. 'And you need to understand that they wouldn't do it at all if they weren't already sure.' He gazed into the space of the kitchen behind her, searching for some detail to fix upon. 'And my mind is fine. Just fine. They set me all these—puzzles. Every day. They test and retest my memory at every available opportunity. You can't imagine just how exhausting that is. But I'm up to it. I never let them down. I can't let them down.'

Kathy remained still for a moment more. Then slowly her breathing returned to her, gently, calmly, and her muscles allowed themselves to untighten.

She ran her hands half-heartedly through her hair, smoothing and patting it in place, then drew the dirty breakfast things towards her, sliding them over the table, and took them to the sink, turning her back to her husband.

'When do you go?'

Frank lowered his eyes to his hands. He began to pick at his nails. 'They'll be here in an hour to collect me.'

'I mean when do you go through.'

Frank frowned. 'Tomorrow, of course. So long as we get the all-clear.'

'I mean—what time.' Kathy filled the sink with fresh hot water. She added more detergent than she needed. She swilled it round till the threads of its green were all gone. 'I want to be up. I want to be thinking of you.'

'Oh.' Frank pondered this briefly. 'Midday. Probably. Could be earlier, all being well. But no later. It's not so important, the exact hour. It'll be when they're, you know, when they're ready. That's what really matters. When they feel it's all—'

He gabbered on for a while but Kathy was no longer listening. She was lowering dirty dishes into the sink. She was immersing her hands in the hot soapy water, wiping away all the grease, the black salty specks.

It was such a simple system. The plates went in dirty and, with a little bit of heat and a little bit of swirling, they came out clean; the water retaining all the muck, holding it to itself. She could see it as the soap suds cleared. She could see the bright globules of fat in glittery suspension beneath the surface. Then, with just a little tug on the chain, out came the plug, and all that grime was sluiced away down the small black hole. It was all so easy. Out of sight. Out of mind.

¶

It was early evening on the following day when they brought Frank back.

The kitchen window was open and it was chilly inside but Kathy sat at the table unmoving, staring at nothing in particular, at the rough dark grain of the wood, at the spatters of unidentifiable dirt on the windows.

She was tired. She was wearing one of her old dresses, its fabric thick and comfortable, a blue shawl loosely draped around her shoulders.

Even when she heard the approach of the car up the long driveway she didn't shift her position.

She heard it come to a stop outside the cottage with its engine ticking over. She heard doors opening and feet on the grit of the path. There was chatter. There was the sound of her husband calling goodbye and the sound of doors thocking shut, the sound of the engine rising as the car set off, then diminishing, then gone.

It was the knock at the back door that made Kathy look up, made her focus on something more than just the space in front of her.

Frank always used to knock before entering. It had been a quirk of his. A politeness. But he'd not done it for months, perhaps not for years. And when the door now opened, and Kathy saw him standing, framed, leaning against the jamb, he didn't come in, not at first, as though he was waiting for something, for her permission maybe.

But Kathy stayed seated, waiting also, and as her eyes adjusted a little more to Frank's silhouette, she noticed he was smiling. Not just smiling, but beaming. Kathy stood up, slowly. She trembled.

Frank stepped inside and when Kathy saw him she couldn't help but take a short breath, almost a gasp. He was beautiful. And when he came closer she could smell him too. His freshness. The natural richness of his scent.

He took her hands in his. He lifted them. He kissed them.

'Would you—' Kathy glanced away from his perfection to the kitchen counter. 'Would you like something to drink? What are you allowed—some tea, maybe? I could make you whatever you wanted. A sandwich, perhaps. Are you hungry? Do you need to lie down? Are there— instructions? Or maybe just the tea for now.'

Frank nodded. His eyes were very bright. He allowed himself to be guided to a chair. He didn't at once let go of Kathy's hands so she had to tug them free of his gentle hold. Frank's own hands stayed raised, so Kathy placed her palms over them and lowered them till they lay flat upon the table. Frank didn't resist.

Kathy turned her back and reached for the kettle, checking it held enough water, setting it going. But all the while she could feel Frank watching her. He was studying her. Scrutinising her.

'I like that dress on you.'

'It's an old one.'

'I like how it falls from your hips. I like the sense of your shape it suggests.'

Kathy glanced up at the ceiling momentarily before turning round, her hands gripping the lip of the counter behind her. When she looked now she didn't see her husband. What she saw was a young man in the guise of her husband. She saw someone serene and childlike, someone she used to know well.

She tried to smile.

'Will you tell me what happened?'

'Of course.' Frank smiled back at her. And his smile was quite genuine. It was broad and unforced. 'They took me apart. Their machine, I mean. *It* took me apart. Down to every atom. Maybe smaller. Who's to say?' He gave a short laugh. 'But I was in a sealed chamber, and the walls, that light—*something* took me apart. It unmade me. And then, in that same instant, it put me back together again. And I didn't know it. Not right away. I couldn't tell if it had worked. I felt like I'd not moved at all. But I had. Because it put me back together somewhere else. A separate sealed chamber. An identical chamber. One only a few yards away. And it did it perfectly. Just like that. It put me together perfectly. Faultless. Just as I should be.'

Kathy's hands gripped the edge of the counter more tightly. Frank saw the motion. His eyes dipped and his smile faded. He stood up. He moved towards her with quick steady steps and he took her hands again, he eased the tension from them and brought them forward, holding them in his own.

'Look at me, Kathy.'

And she looked at him.

'Listen to my voice.'

And she was listening.

'Is it anyone other than me? Could it be?'

Kathy gave a little shake of her head. She looked down again. She was going to lean forward and slip her arms around his waist and hug him. At least, she was considering it, she imagined doing it, the movement of it, the feel of it. But Frank suddenly laughed, loudly, and drew away from her.

'Oh, but I gave them quite a shock!' He went back and seated himself at the kitchen table. His eyes were shining as he recounted his tale. 'When I came out. When they opened the door, oh, you should have seen their faces. There was blood everywhere! Over my lips, my chest. All down my front, in fact. I was a little disoriented, of course, a little dizzy, so I hadn't noticed. And I was trying my best in that moment to counter the dizziness, to hold myself upright. That's all I was really thinking about. Just trying to stay standing up. Of course, as it turned out, it was only a nosebleed. That's all. You know how I used to get them? When I was younger? A sign of good health, we always said. Just life overflowing. But *they* didn't know that. Blood is blood, after all. They thought it was due to some terrible accident. But nope, nothing worse than a nosebleed. I guess it must have been the excitement. I was so nervous when I went in. I couldn't help it. But I've got a lot of blood. Yes. A *lot* of blood. Enough to spare a little.'

The kettle was rumbling. Its whistle was starting to sound. Kathy switched it off at the wall but made no further move to make the tea.

'And they checked you over?'

'Naturally.'

'Thoroughly? Ran all their tests and such?'

'Yes!' Frank beamed again. 'I'm fine. Really. Couldn't be better.'

'And—you have to go back soon?'

Frank frowned, but the smile stayed. 'You know I do.'

'To go through again.'

'That's the plan. This was just the first test. It wouldn't be much of an experiment to run the procedure only once.'

'But you don't have to, do you? You could say no. You could say you didn't feel well. They wouldn't make you do it if you told them that. They couldn't.'

Frank looked at her quizzically. 'But I do feel well. That is, I certainly don't feel unwell. And I couldn't exactly lie—'

'I don't want you going through any more.'

There was a pause.

'But honey, you know I have to. I must.' Frank came forward once again and put his hands on Kathy's hips.

'It wouldn't be fair to them if I didn't. They've invested so much in me. In us. I don't want you to be worried, but I can't refuse them. How would you suppose I—'

'When do you go?' There was a quiet urgency in Kathy's voice, a nervous quivering. She swallowed. 'Go through again, I mean.'

'It's not scheduled for another week.' Frank considered this. 'Could be sooner, I suppose. I can check. But why? What's got you so spooked?'

'I—I don't know. It was just—' Kathy turned about. She stared at the kitchen tiles. Their gleaming white. 'It's probably nothing.' She reached out towards the wall socket and flicked the switch back on. In an instant the kettle began its rapid reboil. 'It probably won't make a difference.' Soon the whistle once more began to sound. 'It can probably wait.'

4. Trial & Error

THE FENCE was twelve feet high. Its fine vertical shafts were of galvanised steel. Springy loops of razor wire ran along its top.

Opposite the fence a steep earth bank descended into a concrete gully. Scrubby trees and brambles grew along the bank's near side; the concrete cracked in places by the slow steady push of new roots.

Beyond the bank, beyond the strip of woodland and the coils of thorny undergrowth, was a housing estate. From here two children, a boy and a girl, made their easy quiet way towards the fence.

It was early-morning bright. The air was still cold from a cloudless night. The children walked in single file along a worn path, winding their way through the trees and between the brambles, their cheap canvas shoes quickly dirtied by loose earth. They took particular care scrambling one at a time down the steep bank because of what they carried with them, something that even a small fall could ruin, something delicate that they passed from one to the other and then back as the safety of the gully was reached.

The fence may have been too high and dangerous to climb but its foundations had long been neglected. In places the concrete had crumbled away altogether, and at the point the children were aiming for there was a hole, a narrow tunnel, burrowed at first by rabbits then widened over the years by larger animals. The children crawled carefully through with their delicate burden, emerging on the edge of the disused airfield, brushing crumbs of soil from their clothes, a toy aeroplane held lightly in the girl's hands, its wings lifting restlessly in the cool morning breeze.

The girl's name was Anita. She was older than the boy by a year. She was taller too. Her hair was long and black and very fine and blew about her face as the two of them stood considering the empty field.

The boy was Lochan. His hair would have looked and acted the same had it not been cut so short that it stuck out straight, brush-like. He stood now with his hands in his pockets, listening to the sounds from the airport buildings at the field's far side, the traffic noise beyond, the intermittent rattle and clang from construction work, the momentary fragments of shouting voices and warning alarms that carried on the wind.

Both children stared especially hard at the tall grey control tower with its wraparound turret of angled windows. They squinted, watching for any signs of movement, for a glimpse of small shadowy stick figures behind the blue-green glass. But there was nothing. And so they stepped forward across the wet grass, on towards the nearest runway strip, a hundred yards or so from the fenceline.

The toy plane bobbed in Anita's hands, catching on any updraught. It was a simple spindly thing, with a slender balsa wood dowel for a fuselage and wings of painted polystyrene foam. Two fixed wheels on fine stiff wire made up the landing gear. A long black rubber band spanned the machine's underside from a hook at its tail to the large red plastic propeller at its nose. The propeller caught the wind too, twitching in the current but halted from turning all the way round by a gentle tension in the band.

The concrete runway was broken. Yellow-flowered weeds pushed through the cracks. Rabbits stalked the verges in search of dandelions, but scattered as the two children approached.

Anita knelt, holding the plane low, and began winding the propeller with her finger, tilting her head to one side to keep her hair from tangling in the simple mechanism.

'You should have brought a clip, or scrunchie, or something.' Lochan leaned forward, watching the winding procedure keenly, watching the waves form and narrow along the length of the rubber.

'I know.' Anita did not look up. 'I already checked. I only have the spare band for this.'

'What about a piece of string?'

'Do you have a piece of string?'

Lochan thought for a moment. 'I've a shoelace? Oh, wait.' He pushed his hand into his pocket and brought out a square of folded fabric. 'How about this?'

Anita paused in her winding and looked at the pale blue cotton handkerchief as it was unfolded in front of her.

'Is it clean?'

'I don't use it.' Lochan held it out to her. 'Always carry. Never use.'

'Okay—you do it though.' Anita went back to her winding. 'Just not too tight, yeah?'

Lochan went to stand behind her, bowing slightly as he gathered up her hair, drawing in the loose strands that fell forward around her ears. He felt Anita flinch and twitch her head back as he tied the handkerchief into a simple raggedy knot he was sure wouldn't slip, but she didn't say anything.

Standing straight again, happy with his handiwork as the loose ponytail flopped onto Anita's neck, Lochan gazed once more towards the airport buildings. The new day's activity had already increased. The traffic noise was louder, horns sounded and engines reverberated from the dark tiers of multistorey car parks.

It was another such car park they were constructing at the other end of the airport. There were cranes. There were dull deep clangs as though from giant items clumsily dropped. There was a sound as of heavy chains being shaken together. Beyond all this Lochan could see the glint of cars moving slowly along the dual carriageway.

'That's probably enough.' Anita held up the toy plane, the band now tightly spiralled beneath its central shaft. 'What do you think?'

Lochan shrugged. 'I don't know. I only tried it in my bedroom. Got it moving. But it bumped the wall too quick. Never actually flew.'

Anita placed the machine on the concrete, holding both body and propeller still before her sudden release, then moving quickly back to give the plane space. The whirring force of the red plastic got the plane going soon enough and it hopped and bumbled at a fair speed along the cracked runway. It showed a definite lightness as it tried to catch the low wind, but there was no clear sign of lift and it came to a stop again after a dozen or so yards.

The children said nothing. They ambled over to retrieve it. They inspected it, turning it over, checking its wheels. Then Lochan set to winding it. He tried twirling his finger very fast around the propeller but he kept slipping and the blades would whirr back and undo his efforts. He realised now why Anita had taken so long. Slow and steady was by far the best approach. The rubber band curled into waves and the waves closed upon one another to form a tight rubber tube, a double helix in which the power for flight resided. When ugly little knots began to form on top of that perfection Lochan stopped. There was no sense in overdoing it.

The wind had dropped. Anita tested the air with a wetted fingertip. This time they tried sending it directly into the breeze. Again it bumped along on its spindly wheels. But this time there was lift. For a moment it rose clear from the ground and wobbled a little on the air before landing softly once more and exhausting the last of its wound-up energy.

Anita laughed and clapped her hand over her mouth. Lochan was grinning. They both ran to collect their machine from its first successful flight.

'It needs more power somehow.' Anita examined the loose length of rubber.

Lochan nodded eagerly. 'Could we use both bands together?'

'Don't think so. They'd tangle or something. And besides, if they both broke we'd have nothing.'

She began winding at once.

Lochan saw no reason to disagree. They could only work with what they had. They could only inch forward bit by bit. Pushing too hard might end in disaster.

There was another loud bang from the construction site, followed by muffled shouts. Lochan looked up at the control tower. It seemed now a lot more imposing than before. He glanced back to the hole in the fence. He felt very exposed. But nothing had happened. There had been no shouts for them to clear off. Even the rabbits had returned silently to the soft grass at the edges of the old runway.

'It used to be illegal to be out on airfields without permission.'

'I know.' Anita's eyes stayed fixed upon the propeller. 'Probably still is. You know, private land and that.'

'And if you were caught running, unauthorised, they could shoot you.'

Anita nodded. 'My dad told me that too.'

'Do you think they did it from the tower?'

Anita shrugged. 'I guess.'

'But did they have, like, a gunman up there? Was it someone's job, do you think?'

Anita paused momentarily and stared into the sky. It was very blue. No hint of clouds. No birds either.

'Well, it'd be down to the security team, for sure.' She went back to her winding. 'Not the air traffic controllers themselves.'

'And did your dad—did he ever have to? Did he even carry a gun?'

'Don't think so. He never said. I don't think it was like that. Not for what he was doing. And it's not like that now. It's all just checks and stuff. Still important though.'

'I know. Like in case someone tries to take a bomb through.'

'Yeah. Although that couldn't actually happen. Not really. I asked but Dad says it's impossible. Mum too. Even if someone were to get that far. Like, right inside? It just—couldn't happen. I don't really get why.'

Lochan nodded. He looked down the long length of the runway. It seemed to slope up slightly at the far end, like a gently curving ramp. Unless that was just his eyes playing tricks. It was such a long way off.

'All this empty space. Bit of a waste, don't you think? You know, it just sitting here. They should put in a bike park. Or cricket pitches.'

'Probably not allowed. Security risk and all.'

'What, like a cricket ball coming through the terminal window?'

'Well, yeah, maybe.' Anita looked up at him seriously, but her finger kept dutifully turning the propeller. She'd got the feel of it now. She could keep the same neat circle going. Not too close to the middle, not too near the tip of the blades. 'More likely just people. Too many, too near the buildings. Everything has to be watched, you see? Monitored. They probably do know we're out here right now.'

'Yeah. I guess so.'

'Yeah, and they probably don't really care because, you know, we're just two kids and they'll have these giant binoculars and they'll be able to see we're not a threat. Not a security risk.'

'And then anyway what would they even—' Lochan gripped Anita's wrist suddenly. 'Hey, careful! You'll overwind it!'

Anita glanced down and saw the knots, the small ugly black knots from where the rubber band had started to double up on itself. But in her hands the tension in the machine felt like it could take a lot more. She continued winding, smiling slyly at Lochan as she did so.

'Oh, so that's the trick!' The boy looked on excitedly. 'We were too gentle with it. It just needs more. More, more, more!'

The knots began to form at random points along the band, but they slowly filled up its full length, and soon they didn't look ugly at all. There was a regularity to them, each forming in the very same stress-pattern as the next, till eventually the entire band looked like just another spiral, double-wound. A spiral upon a spiral. As though it had at last reached the configuration it had always meant to assume.

Anita placed the taut machine carefully on the ground, glancing up often and making tiny adjustments to the plane's forward angle. She was neat in her release, taking both hands away sharply, but whether from the strength of the breeze in that moment or perhaps from having too much power, the plane didn't fly. It bounced for a while over the uneven ground, toppled forward onto its propeller and, twisting itself round and flopping onto its back, buzzed angrily as it tried to release the energy still stored in its band.

Lochan dashed over and stuck his finger into the plastic blades of the propeller to stop it spinning. It only stung a little. The machine became still and silent, wholly compliant.

'It's this rough ground.' Anita stubbed the sole of her shoe against the runway. 'Would've been fine for jumbo jets and their big rubbery wheels. Would've seemed smooth to them.'

Lochan nodded. He'd already begun the long process of winding again. 'Like an ant crawling over sand.'

'Like a what?'

'You know, like sand on a beach would for us feel fine and smooth and soft and all that, but for an ant or some tiny beetle or whatever it'd be like crawling over tough rocky terrain. Just like our little plane over all these bumps.'

'Oh right, yeah—like that.'

The winding continued.

Anita looked on attentively, watching Lochan's slowly twirling finger and the rubber band's gradual bunching, as though this was the most crucial aspect of it all, as though Lochan might somehow get this part wrong and how simply everything depended on this calm yet meticulous preparation.

But Lochan didn't look at what he was doing, instead he glanced vaguely upward, gazing out over the airfield. The morning was growing warm with the sun. The dew shone silver on the wide expanses of grass and glittered as the droplets slowly evaporated, each one diminishing, leaving a rich green beneath.

'I used to think they'd sell it.' The boy stared wide-eyed into the middle distance. 'So much land. They could put houses on it. Loads of them. Think of all the people that could live here. All together.'

'They won't though.' Anita itched to take over the winding from Lochan. It wasn't that he was doing it badly, she just felt she could do it better. 'Dad says it'll go to make more buildings, eventually. Terminals. Car parks. That sort of thing. Anything of benefit to the travelport.'

'New facilities.' Lochan nodded, still staring dreamily ahead. 'A hotel, maybe. For anyone all set to travel.' He looked up at Anita. 'Would you ever use it?'

'Well, no. I live just over there.'

'Not a hotel. The travelport itself. The network.'

'Oh.' Anita considered this briefly. 'No. Can't afford it.' She sniffed, rubbing her nose with the back of her hand. 'And anyway, nowhere to go.'

'But your mum *and* your dad work there.'

'So? Doesn't mean we get free tickets.'

'It can't be that expensive, can it? I mean, what does it really cost? Like, how much energy does it use up?'

Anita shrugged. 'Dad says the price will get lower, eventually. But with all the new equipment, and all the precautions, etc. It's supposed to be real quick and that, but the queues are horrendous. Mum never stops.'

'Is it true you have to be naked? To go through, I mean.'

'Yeah, it's true.' Anita nodded. 'That's what Mum does. She looks after people before they get sent. Explains how it works. Safety measures. What to expect. All that stuff. She has to repeat those same things, over and over, all day long. Even to people who use it regularly. You know, business folk. It's the law. She finds it so so boring. And still she has to go on smiling. All day long. But, yeah, I know what you mean, I wouldn't like that part either, having to be naked in front of strangers.'

'Yeah, but, if it's your mum, that'd be okay, right?'

'Why? Would *you* not mind being naked in front of my mum?'

Lochan swallowed and looked back down at the plane in his hands. Without noticing, he'd stopped winding it, he couldn't tell for how long. He got back into it with renewed energy. Anita's mum was very pretty. It was part of the job.

'But if that's what everyone does. If everybody else is doing it. If, you know, it's accepted. Like going to the doctor, or like being unconscious for an operation or something while people prod you and probe you, then maybe it's okay. The naked bit, I mean. I'm not sure about the rest of it. I'd be worried. Worried things might, you know—go missing.'

Anita snorted out a laugh. 'What, you mean like your balls?'

Lochan didn't laugh. His face flushed, yet at the same time he felt a little surge of excitement, as though the idea was somehow appealing. Or perhaps it wasn't the idea itself, so much as who was suggesting it.

'Yeah, no. What I meant was—something like a finger, actually.' Lochan held up the toy plane by way of explanation, his finger still slowly twirling, the odd sensation of the propeller's fine blade circling his skin, round and round, without ever slicing through. 'You know, like just your little finger, like it just not being there when you come out the other end, like it's been forgotten, left out when you're all—put back together and stuff.'

Anita squinted. 'I don't think that could ever really happen though.'

'Sure it could.'

'Maybe theoretically, but even then—'

'No, but, if theoretically then, yeah, it could actually happen, for real.'

'I don't think so.' Anita frowned, pressing her lips together. 'It'd mean a loss of data. And data is always retained, you know? It's constant. It's not like it could ever just leak out of the cables.'

'Well then, some of the data could stay in the cables. Still retained, still constant, just not all coming out at once. A bit left behind in the pipes. Forever whizzing round.'

Anita considered this. 'But there aren't any stories of it happening. We'd have heard. It'd be in all the papers.'

'But it'd get covered up though, wouldn't it? They'd know immediately, of course, when you came out with a bit missing. And they'd shuffle you away, and they'd promise you loads of money, if you kept quiet.'

'Well—I guess so.' Anita smiled. 'Might even be worth it to get a big payout. Might never have to work again. Like you could live in total luxury all your life. And all for the loss of a little finger.'

'Or a toe maybe. Better to lose a toe.'

Anita had been watching the progress of the rubber band. Now she reached forward and took the aeroplane from Lochan's hands. He gave it over without question, taking care to keep the propeller from spinning free.

Anita had been thinking very carefully about this next flight. She'd had an idea. She held the machine at shoulder height and waited for a drop in the wind. When it came she released the blades and ran a few steps forward down the runway before giving the plane a little shove into the air.

This time it really flew. It flew beautifully. And not simply gliding. The children watched in silence as the propeller spun fiercely, powering their little machine through the air on a gentle roundabout course, lifting and falling slightly on the breeze. They were amazed at just how long the propeller kept spinning, at how much power all their winding had put into one simple long black rubber band. And when that power was exhausted, down came their plane, very gently, to land nose first in the short damp grass beside the runway.

The two children ran over to collect it. They checked it. They began winding again at once, Anita this time taking up that vital duty.

'Must have been up for a minute, at least!'

'Nah, it only *felt* like a minute.'

'But it did fly a long time.'

'Yeah, but like a minute is way longer than that.'

Lochan went silent for a while, counting in his head.

At length he nodded, sure of himself. 'I think maybe like fifteen seconds then?'

'Fifteen's good. We can try to beat that, next flight.'

'And we'll time it properly.'

'Yeah, and then try to beat that too.'

'Yeah.'

They both concentrated on the winding; Lochan's watching being just as intense as Anita's twirling. It was crucial. It being that part of the procedure in which nothing much happened but on which everything depended.

Till Lochan found himself looking past the plane, staring through it at the ground below.

They were now standing on a bit of the runway that looked to have been recently repaired: a long strip of smooth black tarmac patching a wide line, a bar across the concrete, from one grass verge to the other. The grass itself grew differently at either end, extending the same line right across the airfield.

'But if the data is really retained—' Lochan followed the direction of the line back towards the airport terminal. 'If it's still in the cables, whizzing round, then I suppose it could come out later. Like maybe—it might attach itself to someone else?'

'That's ridiculous. What, like I could go through and come out with an extra finger? I don't think so.'

Lochan considered this silently for a moment.

'Better that than if you go through and end up with my balls.'

They both laughed. So much so that Anita lost her grip on the propeller momentarily. They laughed, and then they looked at each other in sudden silence, and they both flushed and turned their eyes away.

Anita wound the band up to its maximum this time. She could feel the tautness in the rubber, its triple-wound row of knots. It was so tight it didn't even feel like rubber any more. She could feel that tension in the balsa frame as well. Everything was tense: a hardness, a sort of oneness, pulling the whole object together. And it was holding.

She gave the machine over to Lochan. He took possession of it with great delicacy. Anita turned her wristwatch round, ready to time the flight.

Lochan faced into the wind. He waited for the right moment. Then he ran as fast as he could, holding the plane two-handed just beside his head, and as he ran he released the propeller, like a relay runner who has to get up to speed before the moment of changeover. And when Lochan released the plane he gave it a good throw, a real boost. And a surge in the wind caught under the wings and the plane went soaring skywards. But in the same instant the wind gusted again and the plane flipped forward and, with all that tension still spinning out through the propeller, powered itself directly into the runway.

The noise when it hit was not loud. There was a lightness to the sound of its splintering, as small parts broke off and skipped away over the concrete, and the tips of the propeller beat the ground, and the plane flapped around helplessly as the remainder of its power ran out.

Lochan had both hands clasped over his head. Anita had frozen, her wrist still raised, her fingertips gripping fiercely the rim of her watch.

Neither spoke as they approached the broken plane, and lifted it together, and turned it gently in their hands, inspecting the damage.

The wheels had come off, as well as part of the tail assembly. That was what they'd seen skittering away at the moment of impact.

'They were only loosely held on anyway. And they're meant to be flexible.'

'Mmm. And I think we can fix the tail.'

'The propeller is scuffed.'

'I think it's probably okay.'

'We could smooth it down with a knife if there are any burrs.'

'Sure. Test the wood.'

Anita tentatively flexed the central balsa wood dowel. There was no sign it had suffered in the crash. She checked the rigidity of the wings too.

'I think it'll be fine.'

'Yeah. I think so. We were really lucky.'

'We just overdid it.'

'I didn't mean it to go up so high.'

'I know. It wasn't your fault. We didn't know.'

'Yeah, and you have to test things.'

They began walking slowly back towards the fence, picking up the other pieces of the aeroplane as they went.

'It makes sense that things go wrong sometimes.'

'Yeah, without things going wrong you can never tell how far you can push it.'

'And we wouldn't have got anywhere without trying.'

'Yeah, and we were so careful, too.'

'I know, and it's not too bad really.'

'No—I think it'll be fine.'

The day was in full swing now. There was a yellow haze over the terminal and a dust cloud over the building site beside it. There was the constant heavy drone of traffic and occasional beeping horns that echoed in the multistorey car parks. And there were voices shouting, and drills, and intermittent sirens, and the deep reverberant clanging of metal on metal.

But the children paid none of it any attention as they cradled the pieces of their toy aeroplane, passing it and themselves through the tunnel under the fence, before scrambling up the dry earth bank and on through the scrubby trees towards the housing estate.

5. Grail Quest

AFTER ALL, she was better than him. Yes, he loved her for so many reasons, the usual reasons, the uncomplicated everyday reasons, but he loved her above all else because he knew that deep down she was a far better person than he was.

And not only deep down, it was there in everything she did. It shone right through her. The more she tried to hide it, the more modest she tried to make herself, the more evident it became. At least to him. There was no competition between them. She was simply better. Always was and always would be.

¶

Her name was Jane.

'Janey, please. No one ever calls me Jane.'

Her name was Janey. He met her at a party in his final year. The party was being hosted by the other girls she lived with. She was sitting apart in her room, in a corner, on her bed. Her bedroom door was open: he went in. He never did like parties.

'I don't much like them either. Well, they're alright. I don't really mind either way.'

She was reading a book, its cover dark grey and lacking a picture. He couldn't quite make out the title.

'Perhaps because it's in German?'

She knew several languages, besides her mother tongue. He knew only one: the language of numbers. She lowered the book to her lap as he came in.

'You can stay if you like.'

He sat at the end of her bed. He asked what the best translation of her book might be, so that he could read it too.

'The best translation of any work is always oneself, wouldn't you say?'

He looked at her quizzically. She seemed quite serious.

'What I mean is: why translate the words into another language that doesn't quite match the depth and complexity and beauty of the original text? So much better, I think, to translate yourself into a person who understands the work the way it was intended.'

And from that moment he was smitten. It was her air of ease that captured him. Her gentle confidence. There was no pretence.

'And of your numbers? What do you hope to do with them?'

Now, for sure, he loved his numbers, he knew them intimately, he understood them intuitively, but he had no particular plan for them. Numbers were just what he was good at.

'Perhaps you could translate yourself too. Into numbers, I mean.'

And yes, that was it, she was right on that score as well. That's exactly what he'd do.

'And then, don't forget, you'll need to translate yourself back. That part is vital.'

And not only himself. He would learn to translate simply everything into numbers. Yes. It seemed so obvious. So clear. He would make it his lifelong goal. His quest.

'It can be your holy grail. If you find it I'm sure the world will be very grateful.'

And so they would be. He was sure of it.

¶

But he had his doubts too. About Janey. About himself. He could never understand why she'd kept with him when he was so inferior to her; the numbers just didn't match up. Even on their honeymoon, as they lay on the hotel lawn in some foreign land looking up at unfamiliar constellations, he wondered if Janey might have been wiser to have waited for somebody else.

'Do I take you? Do you take me? They're just words. It's just a ceremony. And a man-made one at that. Which does lower its integrity somewhat. What God feels about it all, however, that's a different matter. You might not see it yourself, but God would surely approve. I'm quite certain he would, having once looked deep inside you.'

And yet his numbers didn't seem to allow for God.

'Perhaps your numbers are themselves God. Or, if you're not so keen on that idea, perhaps your language of numbers is the same one God uses.'

Perhaps it was. Perhaps it had been the original language of all mankind, and would be again someday. A language that would set them on a sure path to the heavens.

'For God so loved the world, he let us wreck it on his behalf. At least that Babel business gave us all a singular purpose. Something to while away the days. Something to strive for.'

Except something went wrong with the numbers. Someone's calculations were not up to standard. And all came tumbling down.

'But all those bright new languages, all those different peoples: that was intended to help us, never hinder. Not just different tongues, but actual different ways of thinking. And, if we could but learn those other tongues, so too we could learn those other ways to think, and in so doing help and understand each other better. And then, maybe, eventually, we could get back to building that enormous tower.'

And yet he felt that for a tower to reach such heights it would need a base of truly mammoth proportions. The task was just too much to contemplate. It was impossible.

'Mankind itself would seem impossible if you were to ask the very first stars, or the cooling rocks, or the teeming seas. Yet here we are.'

¶

His work at the institute was in analysis. He was involved with a device that could see right inside a person and read every part of them without them needing to be opened up.

He worked on the numbers side of things. The team had already created the basic unit by which any object could be looked through, but how the device understood and decoded what it saw, and how it relayed that information effectively back to the operator, was where his numbers came in. Down at that level of analysis everything was numbers.

It was his task to convert all these numbers into a useful diagnostic readout.

'An interesting word: *diagnostic*, wouldn't you say? Di-agnostic, dia-gnosis, diag-nose. The *dia* is the *through* part. But not just *through*, there is a sense of wholeness to it. And the *gnostic*, the *gnomic*, the *gnome*, well, that's the understanding part, the knowing part. Except, who can really be said to know anything for sure? One can only really judge, after all. So, no matter how good your diagnosis, it's always and only a judgement, a best guess. And the quality of the judgement is only as good as the quality of the judge. But who will judge the judge to see if he, or she, or it, is up to scratch? There's only one true judge, and he keeps things pretty close to his chest. At least in so far as these number matters go.'

And yet, that was the very idea: to make a machine that was more than simply a judge. To make a machine that was infallible in its knowing. A machine where the diagnosis would be quick and clean and full and absolute.

'Not much good in knowing the problem if you don't know a way to fix it.'

Perhaps. But they had to start somewhere. And for the machine to fix the problem too? All in one go? Well, that would require something else entirely.

'That would be the real holy grail. That indeed would be worth striving for.'

He didn't doubt that she was right. But all too soon he became distracted in his quest. Next door at the institute, in a wholly separate department, they were playing with dust, with particles, with microscopic elemental specks. And they were sending them down coils of wire, down long fine loops, to end up somewhere other than where they had started, yet bodily no different than before.

But how could they be sure their transported specks were truly the same specks when their structure was identical to any other speck? And how could they be sure, when the specks were so tiny and the wire so thin, that they weren't travelling the coils in anything other than the usual way, or that anything exceptional was happening at all?

What they needed was to send bigger objects: a grain of salt, a sugar cube, a small steel ball. By their calculations it should be possible, but their machine had limited depth-analysis. In this, he thought he might lend them a hand.

When at home he told Janey all about these new developments she became suddenly very serious.

'How much do we have? Moneywise. What's our current number?'

He showed her their most recent statement.

'Then buy as many shares in the institute as you can. As many as we can afford. Buy them quick. Even if it's only a handful. But do it soon. Do it tomorrow.'

And he did, because Janey always saw so much deeper than anyone else. All those languages, all those ways of thinking: she didn't need a special analyser, she didn't need his numbers to decode the world around her or the people she might meet. She saw right through people, and things, and past-present-future, with merely a glance. She knew what he was thinking, and what he would do, and what the outcome would be when it was done.

'It's like I always say: the more languages talking to each other, understanding one another, the more varied the manner of thought.'

And so the two technologies were married.

¶

The institute came and installed a pair of oven-sized units in his basement for him to experiment with. And he sat, late into the evenings, wondering how he could make this new machine better understand the matter it was transporting.

Janey had recently discarded a favourite loose-knit cardigan due to an unsightly pull in one of the threads. He decided to use it as a test object. Its complex organic woollenness coupled with the repeating loops of the weave made it an interesting candidate for analysis.

He put it into one of the units and then examined its softness, its luxuriousness, its cardiganness, once it had appeared in the unit opposite. It hadn't changed. Even the pulled thread was itself just as it had been.

'The problem with translation is often: do I alter, or even correct, what I translate so that it makes better sense in the new language? or do I hold as close to the original as I can and so muddy the meaning? What is it to understand a thing over and above it merely being the thing it is? More importantly, though: I'm still not going to wear it.'

And that was indeed where he was going wrong with the machine. He was trying to teach it to understand when it didn't need to understand. It needed only to do. To analyse, unravel, re-form. No understanding. No changes to be made. No improvements.

¶

But the work at the institute suddenly stalled, just as they felt they were getting somewhere, and all because of the risk of weaponisation. As soon as they'd got it working, effectively, unerroneously, they had to stop the whole programme, at once.

Everybody knew that if a system like this had the potential to be abused then it would indeed be abused. Send through a bomb. Send through a man with a bomb. Or a gun. Or a knife. Send it direct: into the heart of the problem. It would make war so much easier. But in such theoretical situations how could the machine ever be made to distinguish and then separate out the component parts? How could such a threat be neutralised?

'It's your machine. Surely you can tell it to do whatever you want. Tell it what not to do. In translation I may have a duty to properly render the original, but I don't have to take on the work. I read the original beforehand, and if I don't like it: I discard it. It simply doesn't get done.'

As straightforward as that. They had a machine that analysed things perfectly, inside and out. The machine didn't need to understand the intent, nor fix the problem, nor even neutralise, but it could recognise. That's what it was best at. And, in recognising what it shouldn't send, it could simply not send. It could reject.

So that was solved.

¶

They found a house in a valley, amid mountains, at the end of a long winding track, far away from anywhere that might conceivably be called local. The house was large and the land it governed was wide, but they could afford it: the upkeep of fences and fields and farmable stock.

They had a daughter. But when they sent her off to school she came right back.

'Because she doesn't get on with the other children. Because she doesn't like the busyness of the outside world. Too many minds, all clamouring. She can't get in. She can't speak to them all at once. But she can see them, all thinking, all that noise. She knows it's there, even if she can't be sure of the words.'

So they schooled her at home.

Her father taught her the facts, the truth of the matter, all that could be reasoned and understood. Her mother taught her opinions and interpretations, the inexplicable aspects of the world, its many mysteries.

¶

Janey drove their daughter to the city, to the art galleries; a necessary part of her education. They both enjoyed the long and carefree drive, the empty roads.

In the city too, there was no great congestion. The traffic lights blinked leisurely, guiding the few road users on their way. Finding parking spaces wasn't hard.

Only the gallery itself was busy: the people milling through each room in silent observation of the art.

'Here is a glimpse of things as they once were. Paintings deemed precious enough never to be transported. They are fixed points. It's the people who are required to do the moving.'

Visitors popped in and out of the gallery spaces, though the overall number at any one time stayed the same.

'One small vestige of sanity in a world whose mind is steadily narrowing, closing in upon itself. A world getting smaller, more cramped, tangled, messy. Less space to breathe, or even think.'

Heading homeward they dipped into the new hypermarket on the city's outskirts. A shop with all seasons of food, from all worldly regions, all shipped in direct. A shop with its own transport hub.

'Don't believe the claims of freshness. Always read the label. One shouldn't eat anything too easily obtainable. A little effort, locally sourced, traditionally preserved, is always best. The extra cost is worth it in the end.'

Leaving, they passed long lines of customers, bags bulging with exotic produce, inching slowly forward to the busy exit booths.

'Making things cheaper won't help them. It only endorses their poverty. It exacerbates how freely they waste what they don't cherish. Not to mention the effect of all that rich food on their unrefined insides.'

¶

The daughter liked guns. She liked their precision, their mathematical aim. She went out often with the neighbouring farmboy and his rifle.

She liked shooting things from afar, especially rabbits, because you could never shoot too many rabbits. No matter the numbers culled there were always enough.

Her parents didn't mind her keenness for bloodsports. If she was happy her father was sure to be happy. Her mother, also, openly approved.

'It's always wise to keep things in check. Matters can so easily get out of hand.'

So when their daughter took a stronger interest in the possibilities afforded by the military her ambitions were met with nothing but encouragement, with easy positivity.

'The world is already such a messy place, it stands to reason something bad will happen. It crinkles up too quickly. You'll need to keep it straightened out. After all, we can't blame anyone but ourselves. We created the means by which the mess could be made, and in so doing created the means by which that mess may be cleared up. It's only right to be prepared. We didn't look far enough ahead. We didn't look deeply enough.'

¶

And when one midwinter day Janey was found to be riddled with cancer, with small discreet tumours spotting themselves at points throughout her insides, she went on pretending that everything was fine, that all was in fact quite normal.

'Because why not? It's a common enough complaint. So many people get it. Why not me?'

And Christmas went on as planned, and expensive gifts were exchanged, such as books with leather spines and colour plates, and fine silver goblets from which to drink mulled wine, and gloves of pale blue cashmere, and embroidered handkerchiefs of purple silk.

'Because it's no good buying things not meant to last. Nor things that can be easily replaced. Or what's the good of giving them at all?'

And then later, after a meal she'd insisted on cooking herself, when they were lounging together in front of the fire, listening to carols in the evening's soft and multicoloured light, her husband wondered out loud just how she managed to stay so calm.

'Because I'm certain that you can, and will, fix it. Your machines will be able to see what the matter is. All you need to do is find a way for them to transport that matter out. Or transport me but leave behind those pieces that are undesirable. It's just what you were always striving for.'

Except it wasn't quite as straightforward as that.

¶

The husband had to try and find a way to undo all his research, to get back to his original trajectory.

He'd made a machine that did not understand what it was hearing when it fired its soundwaves in and through and back.

All it could do was listen and repeat.

'Écoutez et répétez. Slushaĭte i povtoriaĭte. Zuhören und wiederholen.'

It had no comprehension of what should, or should not, go into composing an object, a thing, a body of any sort: of what components were right, or good, or best.

Its approach was holistic. Whatever it saw was just how it should be. There was a purity in that. A truth. Just like the truth and purity of numbers.

'But surely through looking it can differentiate. It knows its language of numbers and particles. With these spots being this, and those being that. If so it can identify what's what.'

It could and it did, and with one further stipulation: if through analysis certain unwanted substances were indeed detected then the body, in its wholeness, could be rejected. That was the extent of its capabilities: to send or not to send. There were no half-measures. No partial transferrals.

'But the machine was made by you. You tell it what it can and cannot do. You command. You control how it operates, how it deals with what it finds. You can make it anew.'

And yes, it should have been possible. And now he put all his effort to that end.

But it wasn't the same as when he'd set out all those years ago. His own mind had become fixed. It had found at length its perfect translation, devoid of any ambiguity. He could not be as fluid in his thinking as once he was.

His numbers too had settled in their ways. He couldn't see how to make the machine do anything other than what it already did. He couldn't make the machine understand that not all matter was to be moved, that some indeed was to be left out.

'What after all should the new gaps be filled with? Scrumpled-up newspaper? Swabs of cotton wool? Premoulded foam?'

¶

Janey left it to him to find the cure, for his long-relinquished quest for the holy grail to carry on now as before. But for all her efforts at brightness, at daily gaiety, sometimes Janey faltered, sometimes she just felt really sick, and she'd withdraw to her room and lie perfectly still, waiting for her old self to re-emerge, to surge up through this new self that she didn't recognise.

'At least, in the end, there'll be one less person around in the world. One less user adding to the mess. A permanent removal from the field. Then maybe someone else can fill the gap I leave behind.'

And the work on the machine continued. And the machine itself became ever more finely tuned, ever more sophisticated in its singular application. Fresh confidence in its overall perception of the nature of things meant people no longer had to suffer the indignity of travelling naked. The noise too became a lot quieter. There was a new sense of precision in the sound, a fine intrusive hum with a laser-like aim, superseding the old scattergun approach.

'Which only means more people want to use it. And so its delays remain about the same. Nothing ever really changes. There's no translation of the human condition. We only think we're moving forward. It only seems that way. And all the while we're really going sideways. Taking a roundabout course. Avoiding the unsightly areas.'

And Janey's husband strived and strived. And Janey's husband failed and failed and failed. And Janey herself became bed-bound, too weak to do more than raise and read the books arranged to be within her reach.

'In the end I can at least translate myself. One final time. Back into earth. And in so doing better know the world.'

¶

Their daughter returned from her service abroad. Her languages made her an excellent traveller, an asset to the military mind: in how to comprehend the enemy.

'How many connections did you make? How many new routes did you find? How many pathways did you open in those people that you met?'

The transporter network made it easier for her to bypass those aspects of the world she didn't much like, to skip over the mess, to go straight to the problem, the matter at hand.

'How much fitter is the world because of you? How many wrongs have you helped to put right? What substance is used to replace what you take out?'

But it was only a fleeting visit. The problems of the world didn't stop just because she was on leave. The ease with which any problem could be identified was only equalled by the ease with which it could spread.

¶

And Janey's husband sat by Janey's bed through all the moments she was awake.

'And when they write your grand biography they'll mention me. They'll say I was the little wife that kept you happy all those many years. I don't mind that. I don't mind that they'll never know.'

But he was certain. Even if they never asked, he'd be sure to tell them. He'd tell them everything.

And while Janey slept he went back to his numbers. It was all he could do, all he was good for. It was what she'd asked of him. He couldn't refuse.

If only he could somehow translate himself, to work harder, to try better, to find what he'd been searching for all this time.

'The trouble is: there never really was a grail. It was a cup. And the cup wasn't magic. Just a cup. And if you search for something that never was there to begin with, no hope can make the search worth all that effort. But there are always other cups, reliable cups, forgotten cups.'

Still he couldn't stop searching. He couldn't go back on his word. He couldn't change himself so readily. He wasn't like her.

Deep down she was always so much better than him. He knew it to be so. She was better than him through and through.

He loved her all the more for that.

6. A Misunderstanding

FLO PUSHES open the black swing-door of the wash-room and ducks inside. Her heart is pounding. She feels dizzy, queasy. For a moment she steadies herself beside the short row of basins, breathing deep and slow. She doesn't have long.

The lighting in the washroom echoes that of the bar: loops of pink and green neon give Flo's face a weird unworldly quality in the large oval mirror.

She unzips her purse and digs around inside, her hand closing upon a small blocky device. She draws it out. It is no bigger than a pack of cigarettes, its thin metal casing a clean matt black.

She ejects the mini cassette tape and holds it up closer to the green light, checking the reels are fully rewound before easing it neatly back into the machine. Softly she snaps the lid shut. With the tip of her finger she slides the tiny red record button upward till it locks in place, then, holding her breath, presses the device to her ear: no hiss of playback, only the faint dull whirr of capstans slowly spooling.

Flo slips the device very carefully into an outer pocket of her purse and zips it in tight. She closes her eyes. She clenches her fists. She breathes out.

For weeks now Flo has been trying to get an interview with the Transport Secretary, but her every request has been refused. She is used to this. She understands this.

She is after all no more than a junior reporter. Not many contacts. Not much clout. Most of her life these days consists in leaving polite but insistent messages for various low-grade officials who never call her back, or else doorstepping nervous men in brown suits as they hurriedly leave the town hall. But Flo steadfastly refuses to be deterred.

Today's confrontation has been worse than most: to have tailed her man all the way to this odd little corner of town only to have him turn on her, in front of other potential sources, in front of other journalists. Had she really pressed him so hard? No. She doesn't believe so. But what he'd said, what he'd called her. It still smarts. It'll take more than a few martinis to shake that off.

And yet the day is not quite lost. For in this out-of-the-way establishment she has caught sight of someone far more interesting than any of the small-town officials she's aspired to interview. Someone much more deeply embedded in the industry. Someone she would never have dreamed of approaching, not officially. Better still, from what she's caught of his conversation with the barman, he's a talker.

Flo glances at her dim dark-eyed reflection. Even she can't see quite who she is or what her intentions might be. From her purse she takes out a small black plastic cylinder and uncaps it, twisting up its soft red wax as she leans in close to the mirror. Her hands tremble. She applies the lipstick thickly. She needs it to show. The same goes for the mascara: the brush redrawn through her lashes till they stand out stiff. A touch of overkill? Perhaps. Or just necessity. She untucks her blouse to adjust her skirt, turning the waistband up to expose an inch or two more thigh. It's worth a shot.

She closes her purse. She checks her watch. Only a couple of minutes have passed. As an afterthought she steps into an open cubicle and pulls the chain before stepping back through the swing-door and on into the bar.

What has she missed? What, if anything, has changed? She scans the room casually as she walks.

A couple quietly smooching in a dingy corner. A loner in a long grey overcoat and dipped hat seated close to the exit, his folded newspaper and untouched tumbler of bourbon laid out before him. Plus the tall elderly man with the high cheekbones and thinning swept-back hair, sitting up at the bar, chatting to the barman.

No one glances Flo's way as she re-enters the scene, but she registers them all. Each one an accessory, a lurid character in a story she is fast making her own.

She resumes her own seat at the bar, a few stools down from the elderly gentleman, her half-drunk martini just as she left it. Carefully, smoothly, she lifts and places her purse on the bar-top, its discreet rectangular bulge angled away from her.

Music is playing. Quiet background music. Jazz or blues or something. She hopes its soft wash of cymbals and brassy nasal whine won't get picked up too much by her recorder. She tries to give the impression of someone lost in their thoughts, staring gloomily into her drink, but all the while her ears strain to catch the thread of conversation.

It's the tall man who's at this moment talking: easily, unconcernedly, confidently.

'—not that the company is squeaky clean. I'm not saying that. Then again, nor am I suggesting there's any dirt to be uncovered, so to speak. That's the wrong way to think of it. What you *could* say is how damn boring they are in their reliability, and that the very reason everyone depends on them, the reason everyone trusts and accepts unquestioningly that the machines, indeed the whole network, works just fine, is because, well— the machines do work just fine. It's that simple.'

'Nah, nah, man. I ain't buying that.' The barman laughs. 'Come on, Mr Jacks. What about all them stories? Everyone knows there's stories. Tales and myths and whispers and all.'

The tall man lifts his palms and smiles. 'Well, there you go. You said it yourself, Carol. Stories are just stories. Nothing more. Ridiculous improbable stories.'

The barman grins. 'Oh, but stories have to come from somewhere, right? They don't just pop up out of the air. You know, out of nothingness.'

Mr Jacks raises his drink. 'You've got me there, Carol. Stories do indeed have to come from somewhere. Can't argue on that score.' He smiles as he sips.

Flo echoes the action, sipping from her own glass as the old man raises his. She doesn't mind if he notices. She sort of hopes he will. Even if they don't consider her part of their little discussion at least she is joining them physically, by presence alone.

'And even if the stories are all, you know, fabricated and that—' The barman, Carol, takes an unlabelled bottle from under the counter and carelessly tops up the old man's glass. 'There's gotta be, like, an incentive for that, don't you think?'

Mr Jacks shrugs, nodding for Carol to continue.

'Well, all I'm saying is how no company that powerful, that all-encompassing, could seriously be that honest, right? That clean. Something's bound to go bad. Law of probabilities. And not just the little things. I mean something big.'

'But if that's so, and I'm not saying it *isn't* so, then why have there never been any reports? Where are the scandals? The disasters?' Mr Jacks sets his glass back down. 'Surely we'd all have heard about it. Surely we'd all know. Law of probability is one thing, yes, but look around. Where's the evidence?'

'Hidden away. Buried.' It's another voice that now joins the discussion: a soft feminine drawl from the other end of the bar. 'Neatly covered over with freshly turned soil, pretty flowers.'

The two men turn to look at the new speaker.

Flo hasn't moved. She doesn't look up. She sits in a half-slouch, gazing at her drink, rubbing her thumb lazily against the wet slope of the glass.

'Because a company that big, that far-reaching, well, it could do whatever it wanted. Wouldn't you say?' Now she turns to look at the two men with a weary smile. 'A company so vital to the world economy, to how the whole world even functions, they could suppress any-thing, just like that. And the governments would all agree. They'd all be in on it. Because that company, that linchpin of modern society, it just couldn't be permit-ted to fail. People would not be allowed to lose faith in the transporter network.'

The two men continue staring at her.

'At least—' Flo lifts her glass, wincing as she downs

what's left in it. '—you might think so. If you believed that sort of thing.'

Flo's heart has begun pounding again. For a moment she feels glad of the pink neon glow from behind the bar, in how it must hide the colour she can feel rushing through her cheeks and around the tips of her ears.

After a brief pause Carol grins. 'Right.' He takes his dark bottle again from under the counter and moves down towards Flo, picking up an empty shot glass as he goes. 'That's right. Yeah. What she said. That's exactly what I've been driving at.' He laughs a little.

A fresh measure poured, a nod from Flo, and the barman resumes his position.

Mr Jacks continues to stare at Flo a while longer, then he too turns back to his drink, hunching his long thin body over the bar.

After a moment he gives a short sniff of a laugh and looks up. 'You know what bothers me most, Carol?'

'Oh, you know me, I wouldn't dare presume to know anything, Mr Jacks.'

'Too much cymbal.'

'Aww, come on now, Mr J. That's a low swing. You know how I feel about that.'

'Nevertheless, I hold that it's true.' The old man sits up straight for a moment, casually raising his glass to emphasise his point. 'Always overdoing it on the cymbal. Too much white noise. A full-frequency static. Random interference. It blots out everything else.'

'Nah, not *blots*, Mr J.' Carol breathes in defiantly, though he keeps on smiling. 'What it does is it *fills*. All them holes left by the other players. You see, it broadens it all out. Gives it a sort of density. An extra weight.'

'I think what you're saying there, Carol, is that it gives it a sameness. A wishy-washy quality. Now, I'm not commenting on the skill of the percussionist, on how well he hits those things, I'm only commenting on what he chooses to hit. It's the *quality* of sound that bothers me. It lacks nuance. It's surface-level stuff.'

'Oh no, sir. I can't be having talk like that. Not in *my* bar. If you carry on in such a way I'm gonna have to make you pay for that last drink. What you've got to understand is how the sound is itself—'

Flo has stopped listening. Her shoulders have sagged. She lets her head droop. If this is some sort of code the two men have switched into she can't decipher it. Unless it means simply that the old man has seen through her ruse and is shutting her out. Or perhaps they've just had enough of her. Either way she feels she's blown her chance and that she ought to go. She places a few notes down next to her empty glass and nods her thanks to Carol. He nods back. She takes her purse from the bar and slides from her stool, turning to leave.

'So, what might your story be, then?'

Flo has barely taken a step. She stops. She swivels round, her mouth slightly open. The elderly gentleman, Mr Jacks, is staring at her.

'Presuming, that is, you do have a story. Which I do indeed presume.'

'Oh, now, I'm sure—you don't really want to hear about that.' Flo swallows. But the man keeps staring at her. Flo is suddenly very conscious of her flaming face, her well-glossed lips, the skirt bunched-up around her waist. She breathes in slowly, imperceptibly, then sighs with practised weariness, as if lazily considering whether to tell him, as if she doesn't much care either way. Her mind races. 'Well, okay, I guess, if you really want to know, then yeah—it was my sister, see. She—' Flo winces. '—well, half-sister really, but, you know— maybe that part's not so important.' She tips her head to one side. 'Anyway, she, well—something happened with her. She went through the, uh, the network, but something went wrong. I mean, she'd been using the system for years, like most folk. But then, well—'

Flo stops. The music has stopped. In the sudden silence Carol is now looking at her too. Flo wonders if the others in the room are also watching; the couple in the corner, the man by the door. The music begins again. Nothing but a pause between tracks.

With the tip of his shoe Mr Jacks pushes the stool beside him a little way back from the bar. Flo hesitates, then comes over. She stops once more, just for a moment, now she's that much closer to this man. Then slowly she steps up and settles herself on the stool.

Mr Jacks watches her all the while. He smiles.

'You'd best get her another, Carol.'

'Sure. Same as?'

Flo nods. As the fresh martini is mixed Flo glances back around the bar. The couple are no longer smooching, but they're sitting so close they may as well be, their foreheads touching, lips moving in whispers. The man by the door, his hat still dipped, eyes obscured, is leaning forward over his newspaper, pen in hand; a crossword puzzle? Perhaps.

The martini is served. Flo smiles her thanks and calmly places her purse up on the counter. Mr Jacks looks down at it. He looks right at the purse and its tight rectangular bulge in the outer pocket. Then he lifts his eyes back to Flo.

'Your—sister?'

'Half-sister, yes. Well, you see, she—' Flo takes a sip from her drink. She takes a deep breath. 'Travelling through the network made her sterile.'

Mr Jacks remains looking at Flo. No twitch. No lifted brow. No shift in his expression at all.

'Oh, sure, I know what you're thinking.' Flo gives a nervous little laugh. 'How could anyone know such a thing for certain? How could they ever tell it was because of the network? Well, I'll tell you. She'd already had one child, see. Perfectly normally. Healthily. A boy. My nephew. Or half-nephew. Or whatever. And he—'

'What's his name?' There is no emotion in Mr Jacks' voice, but his eyes are locked on Flo, scrutinising her with uncomfortable intensity.

'And why should that—' Flo sits back suddenly, frowning. 'He's—Alex. Well, Alexander. But I don't see how—'

Mr Jacks gives a little shake of his head and glances away. 'I just wondered, that's all.' He smiles. 'Go on.'

'Right, well—' Flo continues frowning for a moment more. 'Anyway, the boy, *Alex*, he's not the problem. He was fine, see. Still is fine. But when she, my sister that is—' Flo pauses. 'Would you like to know her name too?'

Mr Jacks shrugs.

'Anyway, when they were trying for a second—nothing happened. Suddenly nothing. She'd had no trouble getting pregnant before. But now, nope, not a thing. Like she'd dried up.'

'I heard that too.' The interjection is Carol's. He is taking glasses from a rack, polishing each one slowly, thoroughly. 'About women drying up. Like, no flow. Like they thought they were expecting, but then nothing. I heard that. I think there's a word for that.'

'No, this was different, because my sister still had her, you know, cycle. Regular as anything. And so she went for treatment, but nothing worked, and eventually they opened her up. They took a slice. Just a very fine slice. What's it called—'

'A biopsy.'

'Right. And it was—well, I don't know how to say it, quite. It was just—tissue. No eggs. Nothing. Like it was blank. Her ovaries. They were—they were just— well, I'm not sure there's a term for it. It was just—'

Flo stops. She glances down at her drink, sullenly, dreamily. But inside she's smiling. She bites her lip to stop the smile from escaping. She's put in a good performance. She can't help but feel pleased with herself.

Mr Jacks is listening intently. He has even leaned in closer to hear Flo's story, to watch her in the telling. Now he straightens again. He sighs.

'No.' He shakes his head. 'I'm afraid that's not at all likely.' His voice is once again expressionless. 'Not with the machines, the network. It wouldn't happen. It actually couldn't.' He takes a sip from his drink. 'I'm sorry to hear about your sister, of course. Terrible thing to happen. Truly terrible. But I can assure you it's not linked to the use of the transporter network. Not in any way whatsoever.'

Flo once more feels the blood rising in her cheeks. Not embarrassment this time but anger. How easily he has dismissed her every word. That she made the story up is irrelevant. He has no right not to believe her. Not after the courage she had to muster to say it at all. Such a sense of superiority infuriates her. She tries to blank it out by pushing on.

'Oh, come on, just because it can't be proved doesn't mean—'

'No.' Mr Jacks stops her with another easy shake of his head. 'The machines work perfectly, you see. Perfect analysis, perfect replication, transportation, integration, or reintegration—or whatever you care to call it. A perfect system through and through. And that, effectively, is the problem.'

'The problem with my story, you mean?' Flo squints. 'Well I say it's only a problem if you accept your own idea about the system being perfect. And how can anyone be completely sure if they only ever—'

'You misunderstand me.' Mr Jacks is holding his glass by the rim. It dangles languidly. 'The very problem with the system is that it really does work. Because, you see, it shouldn't. Because, fundamentally, it can't. The concept itself is, quite frankly, incredible. Preposterous really. No one in truth understands how it actually does whatever it does.' He gives a little sniff of a laugh. 'There's your problem right there. They only know, and only then by the evidence of experience, which doesn't count for much, that the system does indeed work. That it is, essentially, faultless. Wherein lies the fault. Wouldn't you say?'

Flo clenches her jaw. She goes to pinch the tiredness from her eyes but pulls her hand away sharply before her fingers touch the mascara. Inadvertently she glances at the bulge in her purse. She turns the glance smoothly into a long blink as she looks up once again at Mr Jacks.

'So—you're saying the system is not altogether safe? Because, if that's so, well, wouldn't that in itself be—'

'Safe? Oh, it's safe alright. In as much as anything is safe. In that being alive is *safe*. I'm just saying that no one knows how it actually works. The whole business is, to put it politely, implausible.'

Mr Jacks drains what remains in his glass. Setting it back down on the bar he nudges it towards Carol who, without a pause, refills it to the measure.

'I—' Flo hesitates. She gives a nervous laugh. She feels she may be missing something. But perhaps it doesn't matter, so long as she can keep the man talking. Sooner or later he's sure to say something useful, something he shouldn't. 'I'm—not sure I quite understand.'

'Oh, don't worry yourself about that.' Mr Jacks gives a reassuring smile. 'No one truly *understands* it. That's the whole issue.'

He leans forward, conspiratorially. Flo matches the movement. Carol too, though he barely moves, seems to focus his presence more intently on the little space this conversation is now about to occupy.

Mr Jacks smiles once again.

'You see, of course, the designers have their theories, yes? Their little philosophies: about particles, about all the various sub-atoms, about the deconstruction and reorganisation of matter, and so forth. And that's all well and good. It's handy to have theories. But that comes after the reality. All that stuff's mere explanation. It's just a shape they've found that fits the ragged hole of their conundrum. It may only fit in a roundabout way, but it does at least fit. Like a toy block going through the wrong window. Or rather: right window, wrong block. Wrong for sure, but still it does go through. And all the while scores of researchers are busy working away, trying to reshape that block, trying to make it fit more snugly. And similarly scores of other researchers are digging around for a different solution, a different toy block altogether. And from time to time they find one, and then for a while that new block seems the very thing they were looking for, it seems like the whole truth, and nothing but. Till they find yet another better block. And then again, later, another. And each block seems to fit. They all fit well enough. Though of course you wouldn't dare go back to using an earlier block. And so long as it's all still working, then, well, none of that really matters. Because they don't really need to know. And the people who use it don't need to know. And the factories too, they need to know least of all. They get their orders, and then they can stamp out this wafer of silicon, or mould that gold-plated contact, based on whatever new template they've been sent. Because anyone can follow a dress pattern, given the right skills. Anyone can convince themselves they know what they're doing, even that they are, in some way, experts. But no one truly gets it, you see? No one really knows. And yet if they thought about it just a little bit more, if they looked beyond what they merely accepted to be true, to what was credible, well, they might realise the whole thing is, if I might be so bold, plainly ludicrous.' Mr Jacks sits up straight again. 'An industry built on a lie. Or, perhaps, to be a little less dramatic—call it a misunderstanding.'

'Wait, are you implying that it—' Flo, too, sits up straight. Her head is swimming. She blinks. She glances at her empty glass. She glances up at Carol but he is ahead of her, placing a tumbler of water down upon the bar, sliding a paper doily under it in the same smooth motion. 'So, I mean, I guess what you're saying is—' When Flo looks back at Mr Jacks he is watching her, steadily. He is waiting. '—is that it does actually work? Or that—it doesn't? I'm sorry to go on, I—just want to be sure.'

'What, take you apart? Strip you right down into nothingness? Send you along a wire as though you were little more than electrons bumping and shuffling into one another? Then put you back together? In the right working order? All those billions of particles? All moving in exactly the right direction, in perfect concordance with one another? All the blood flowing just right? The cells each suddenly restarted, just like that? The intricate patterns of your thought, continued, just where you left off?' Mr Jacks leans his head to one side. He squints at his patient listener. 'Do you know, to put it one way, just how much energy that would require? How much raw power? It's impossible. Everyone with a little bit of sense knows it's impossible. It's a dream. A fantasy.'

'I have actually—you know, seen them work, though.' Flo's voice is cautious. She clasps her glass of water in both hands. 'They do work. Many a time I've even—I know people who've used them, who use them regularly. I've seen these people go. I've seen them come back.'

'Ah, but did you really see them?' Mr Jacks gives a wide thin smile. 'Or did you simply believe that you did?

Is that what you saw happen, or only thought you saw happen, precisely because that's what you expected to happen? That that was what you were led to believe and so, in your mind, that's exactly what did happen.'

'I—what?'

But Flo is unable to fully voice her confusion. There has been an interruption. The couple who've been so absorbed in one another have come forward. They have stepped out of the quiet wash of jazz music, out of the dimness fringed with greenish pinkish light, and now they are perched up at the bar, ordering more drinks.

Flo has turned her face away. She sets her glass of water down. She inclines her head. She does not want the couple to think this is an open conversation.

The couple are young. The tall skinny boy takes care of their order, watching Carol intently as each drink is mixed. The girl is short and rounded. She leans back against the bar, beside Flo.

Flo, feeling that she's being watched, turns her head a little. The girl is looking right at her and smiling broadly. Flo gives a short smile back. This makes the girl grin. She rolls her eyes knowingly at Flo. Flo frowns, but the girl shrugs and gives a short nod towards the bar's exit. Flo glances that way, briefly, but no one new has come into the bar. The only other customer is still sat at his lonely table, still pondering over his newspaper, his puzzle, still in his raincoat and hat, as though he might suddenly leave, at any moment, as though he has only dropped by.

Flo turns back for further silent explanation but the girl seems to have lost interest and is now attending fully to her boyfriend as he carries the drinks back to the private gloom of their corner table. Flo watches them go.

'There is of course another theory. Would you like to hear it?'

Mr Jacks is watching her again, just as intently as before. Flo doesn't know what she wants any more. This has not been the direction of discussion she was hoping for. She nods politely. Mr Jacks continues eagerly.

'That there's no actual travel involved in the process. Well, not as such. The machine destroys you at one end, truly, utterly, and the other machine, at the other end, doesn't exactly re-form you so much as build a brand-new version of you, an identical version to the one that, just an instant beforehand, ceased to exist. So there's no actual flow of you in between.' Mr Jacks pauses briefly. He laughs. 'No flow at all.'

Flo does not laugh. Flo is starting to feel more than a little uneasy about the situation. Flo feels she is, perhaps, not the person she thought she was. But if Mr Jacks is in any way aware of this, he doesn't show it.

'I'm quite keen on this theory, you know. It feels somehow more plausible. In that you don't actually travel the wires. Not *you* you. Not in particle form. Only the information of you is sent. So in a manner of speaking the you that comes out the other end isn't you at all. And yet it is. Because what does it matter what matter has gone into making the new you. As long as everything's in the right place, in precisely the right order, and direction, and speed, then it's just as much you as that other you was really you. Or arguably so.'

'And—is that what you think really happens?' Flo clutches vainly at the suggestion. 'Because I don't think people would like that. If they knew. If they thought it wasn't really them. If they thought they'd first been—'

'But it *would* be them, don't you see? So long as the replication is accurate. Just as a body replaces its cells, its atoms, over a period of years. We all do it, all the time. The person we were yesterday is not composed of exactly the same stuff as the person we are today. Just as we can't be sure we are the same person who wakes up each morning, unless we stay awake all through the night. We can't tell for sure what happens in that intervening period. That void of sleep. The muddle of dreams as our thoughts are reorganised, reconstituted. But what that makes of us when we awake, well—'

Mr Jacks spreads his hands and shrugs. Flo opens her mouth to speak, to bring the conversation back to her original aim. She has to at least try. But as she searches for the right words another voice gets in before her.

'I too have a theory. A good one. Might even say it's true.' It's Carol. He is standing with both hands flat to the bar. He has a serious look. 'If you don't mind my interjecting.'

Mr Jacks motions for him to go on.

'I've been thinking, and what I think is—it's kind of like time travel. You know what I'm saying?'

Flo feels her eyes widen. She tries to hide this look of dismay by transforming it seamlessly into one of curious intrigue, tipping her head to one side, nodding and smiling in general agreement.

'You know? Like what Mr Jacks said about the re-organisation of matter? Well, that sounds a lot like time travel to me. Because all that reorganising, that re-constituting, that's from an earlier state, right? I mean, maybe only a fraction earlier, because sure, it may all happen at the speed of light, like electricity, or radio waves, or whatever, shooting down the wires like that. But it's still a speed, it's still a gap of time, right? And so what actually *are* you during that time? Because if you are when they put you back together exactly what you were when they took you apart, then what have you been in that tiny gap between? So like, when you're travelling, if we can call it travelling, do you really exist at all?'

'Oh, I like that.' Mr Jacks wags an encouraging finger at the barman. 'That's good, Carol. You've excelled yourself.'

Flo nods again. She refreshes her smile. But she remains silent. She feels heavy. She puts extra effort into sitting up straight.

'Sure, and if you could then, like, maybe extend that gap in between?' Carol is beaming. He addresses his grand idea equally to Mr Jacks and to Flo, turning to look at them both with his eyes shining. 'If you could, like, slow it down? Like through even more loops of wire? Like massive long coils of that same cabling going round and round for millions of miles?'

'Like a giant resistor! Yes!' Mr Jacks thumps his fist on the bar in approval.

Carol shrugs. 'Well, I don't know about that, but sure, I guess—a resistor. Anyway, if you could really slow it down, staying in the wires all the while, then bam! there you'd have it—time travel.'

'But only forwards, mind.' Mr Jacks points at the barman. 'With such a system you could never go back—to an earlier era, a younger you.'

Carol considers this. 'Sure. Only forwards. I guess.'

Flo slides from her stool. She stretches a little. She looks at her watch. 'I like it, Carol. It's a fine theory.' She reaches for her purse. Her hands are shaking. She doubts anyone will notice. 'But I'm afraid I need to be getting along.'

'Oh, I am sorry.' Mr Jacks does not look especially sorry. 'Here, we've been prattling on for so long, we've not come close to resolving your problem with Alice.'

'It's fine, I—' Flo stares at him suddenly, the strap of her purse half-hoisted to her shoulder. 'Who?'

'I'm just saying we never resolved the question of your sister's infertility. Though I stand by what I said, that it was not in fact the fault—'

'I—don't have a sister called Alice.'

'Really?' Mr Jacks looks momentarily perplexed. 'Then who is it I'm thinking of?' The perplexity soon evaporates. 'In any case you really can't go blaming the transporter network given that those who profess to be—'

'Mr Jacks, please.' Flo has had enough. She realises now that she has made a mistake, that she has picked the wrong man after all. She realises now that he is nothing less than a crank, a nutcase. It isn't that what he is saying makes no sense, it is that him saying the network makes no sense in itself makes no sense. The idea angers her and for a moment her rising anger cuts through the haze of her evening's drinking. 'If you're honestly suggesting they don't understand how their own machines work, that they never knew, then really I'd say they are very much to blame. There would have been tests. There are always tests. And with those tests there would have been accidents, no? Things would have to go wrong before they went right. And things could still go wrong now. People could be—changed. The network could fail. And furthermore—'

'Oh, no no no. Nothing like that.' Mr Jacks taps the bar with his forefinger. 'That's not the issue here. That's not the problem at all. The real issue is our acceptance of a system that nobody quite understands. A system that doesn't even make sense. And yet we all trust it. We all buy into it. It's a matter of blind faith. We use it because we're told it works. We accept that. We have no reason not to believe it. And now we're locked into that system. We'll go on using it no matter what anyone might say. So what does that make of us? It's not about what the machine does or doesn't do to us as we go through it, but rather: what has the very existence of the machine already made of us? What people have we become? It rules us. It orders the way we live. We allow it to do so. We invite—'

'Please stop, Mr Jacks.' Flo has held up her hand. The trembling is now quite evident. She doesn't care any more. 'Please. Just—stop.' She takes a deep breath. She will try one last time. 'Are you saying that in all these years, and with millions, if not billions, of people using the network, putting themselves through these machines again and again, that you've never heard of even one serious incident? Not one fatality? Not one— something? Anything?'

Mr Jacks stares at her. He gives no indication he is about to speak. It's Carol who breaks the silence.

'I think what Mr Jacks is trying to say—' The barman's voice is low and steady. '—is that it's not about the machines not working, it's about them not *needing* to work.'

'What?'

'The whole network. It's not necessary. Aside from maybe, you know, employment. Though I guess all it's really doing is replacing one employment with another.'

'What?'

'He's quite correct.' Mr Jacks has rejoined the debate. His manner is calm, sober. 'We'd be better off simply pretending, wouldn't you say? You know, we could use cardboard boxes and taut string.'

'Right.' Carol nods heavily, seriously. 'Just use your imagination.'

'Swap places for a day.'

'A whole lot less fuss.'

'All this rigmarole. And for what?'

'Sure, we may get to places a mite quicker.'

'And we're all very happy with that.'

'Or that's what they want us to think.'

'But what do we truly become if we persist—'

'Gentlemen.' Flo holds up both hands this time. 'Thank you. It's been a blast. It's been—enlightening. But I have to go. I'm leaving. I'm going home because, to tell you the truth, though I think you both already know full well, this is all nonsense.'

'That's it exactly!' Mr Jacks smiles broadly. 'You know, Carol, I think she may be coming round to our way of thinking.'

Flo turns on her heel. One step forward and she spins round again. 'You know what? I thought, I really hoped, I might just get a straight answer.'

'Everyone starts off that way.'

'I thought that perhaps you of all people—'

There is a pause.

Mr Jacks raises his eyebrows. 'Go on?'

Flo opens then shuts her mouth. She turns and heads for the door. She approaches the man in the raincoat and hat, his head bowed, his drink undrunk, still scribbling into his newspaper. He shifts the paper over as Flo passes by, covering his right hand. He doesn't look up.

Outside the night is cold and damp. A narrow red-brick stairway leads up to the street. Flo halts on the pavement and swings her purse round, unzipping the front pocket and drawing out the small black dicta-phone. She stops the recording and, firmly, ejects the tiny cassette.

She grits her teeth. She has a good mind to drop the damned thing in the gutter and put the whole sorry evening well and truly behind her. Instead she merely sighs. Such items aren't cheap. The tape goes back in the machine. Flo presses rewind.

The street is very quiet. No one will be out at such an hour. Flo unfolds a small tatty-edged map from her pocket. It shows there should be a public booth just two streets away. So long as it hasn't been vandalised, and so long as she has the right change, Flo could be home again in as little as five minutes.

In her hand the tape stops rewinding and the machine clicks itself off, ready to record another story, a more convincing story, a story Flo's readers might actually want to hear. Flo zips the device back into her purse and steps forward, making her unsteady way along the street.

7. Last Suppers

HE WAS a boy who took everything apart. He would unstitch bears to get at the growler, curious over the source of each unhappy moan. He would ease the limbs off action men to see how the ball-and-socket joints were fixed. Given a puzzle pre-muddled he'd dig a kitchen knife between the blocks and, breaking the object apart, lay all the individual segments out, to reassemble again in just the right order.

His parents thought this behaviour was not unusual, they'd tell themselves he was just a typical boy, always inquisitive, never resting, never taking anything for granted; even though other parents did not report the same of their children.

His first computer he built himself out of various electronic goods others discarded as junk, upgrading it over the years as further unwanted items were discovered. To most the machine looked ugly, a hotchpotch of parts, with exposed circuit boards and bare-ended wires and soldering points on which a loose sleeve might catch. With this in mind his parents hesitated whenever it came to buying new devices for their home, for fear such items would end up being pulled apart and plundered. But this was a misplaced worry. Nothing they bought ever failed. Or if it did it wasn't because of their son. If any issue did arise: he'd find the fault, he'd fix it.

And so it was, eventually, as with nearly every other household, they bought a family transporter unit and had it installed.

¶

'And it's them you blame? Ultimately? Your mother and father?'

The man was very large, dressed all in black. His suit and shirt were so deep a black you couldn't see where one fold of cloth overlapped another. The black tie and black collar and black neck above all blended together into a singular shadow. As he talked his broad head swayed slightly, as though its great weight was precariously balanced. He stood in the corner of the room where the light was at its dimmest. His eyes were not visible, a pair of dark glasses obscured them, though the small round lenses stayed fixed upon the boy all the while the man spoke.

'My parents? Ultimately? Hmm. I don't think so. If I tugged on that thread where would it all end? At my birth? Theirs? At the beginnings of the whole human race? At existence itself? No. I can't allow myself to think like that. I don't even blame the manufacturers. I don't suppose I blame anyone. Not even me. Why would I? Blame seems, hmm, it seems the wrong word somehow.'

The boy was tall and pale, with spindly limbs and long dark hair that ran in soft wavy locks to the tops of his shoulders. He sat on his wooden stool with his slippered feet perched on the chair's upper rung so that he could lean his forearms easily upon the points of his knees. He wore a pale blue boiler suit. It fitted him badly, even after being turned up at all four cuffs and cinched around the waist with a canvas belt. He didn't look directly at the man as they spoke. He would gaze at the opposite wall, or the floor, or the caged light-fitting above, addressing his words to the air.

'I understand that's what they want: someone to blame. That's up to them, I suppose. And maybe, yes, maybe they're right to want it.'

'You don't have to say such things. There is nothing you need to believe any more. Nothing to accept.' The man shifted. For a brief moment he leaned forward from his corner and the lights overhead caught upon him but didn't soften the blackness of his form, they only made that blackness seem more stark, cutting a man-shaped hole in the paler surround. He settled his body back against the wall. 'You have no obligations. Repentance will not change the situation. They cannot be seen to go back on their word. This is not a matter of mercy. It is one of example. Its intent is to deter.'

The boy gave a short sniff of a laugh. He swivelled his eyes surreptitiously upwards, glancing at the ceiling corners, marking out the fine black holes: microphones, optics, etc. He knew he was not speaking in confidence. He knew they'd be eager for him to let slip something of use. But there was nothing to let slip. Nothing more than what he'd already told them.

On the table in front of the boy was a clipboard. It held a single printed sheet. A menu. He looked down at the long list of options, an empty tick box standing ready at the end of each line.

'And if I don't want anything on here?'

'It is but a guide. Some can't think what to choose, can't think of food in such a circumstance. A bit of prompting, a little triggered recognition, they start to recall those things they used to like. Or perhaps they see something they always wanted to try.'

The boy unclipped the sheet and turned it over. Uncapping the felt-tipped pen provided, he began writing down his choice.

¶

The new unit was to be housed in their old walk-in larder. Installation was quick and efficient. A team of men came and assembled the apparatus on the kitchen floor before sliding the whole chamber very slowly into its allotted space, as easily as if they were fitting a new washing machine. Cabling was laid, checks were made, and soon it was all up and running and ready to go.

The unit fitted its hole very snugly. It would be hard for the boy to get at if he wanted a proper look, but not impossible. He showed little interest in the device for a few weeks, aside from occasional use. But when his parents had gone out one afternoon, and knowing they'd not be back for several hours, he wheeled his ungainly computer into the kitchen, located the service port on the transporter unit, and plugged in.

As simple as that. He didn't even try to mask his actions. He wasn't going to do anything. He only wanted to look.

He sat for an age, watching the data flow by on his screen. It was a strange language, but there were aspects he recognised, patterns that revealed a clear linguistic structure. So the boy sat and watched, and he learned, and he saw after a while that something about the coding was not quite right.

¶

'You saw a fault. You wished to correct it. This is understandable. Many have done worse.'

'Not really a fault. Not as such.'

The menu had been taken away and several stiff foil containers now lay upon the table, each with a thin cardboard cover. The boy was leaning forward, examining symbols scribbled between the oily stains that leaked through from beneath. He hovered his hands over each container in turn, moving his palms between them, never touching foil or lid. Then he sat back again and folded his arms.

'You don't want to eat?'

'It still has a bit of a buzz to it. I prefer it to sit awhile.'

'Does that make a difference?'

'Hmm, well, no. I suppose not.' The boy sighed and leaned forward once again. 'It's just something I've always done.'

He began bending back the foil corners, digging in the tip of a plastic spoon to prise up each lid, laying them neatly in a pile at the edge of the table.

Steam rose from each dish as it was uncovered.

¶

Nothing was said about his interference with the unit. His parents hadn't noticed. No one came knocking.

At the next opportunity he took the machine itself apart, but only a little. He levered it gently upward and teased it from its hole, exposing the rawness of its sides, like a mollusc part-scooped from its shell. He was careful that nothing was disrupted, that no one would know it was being dismantled or examined. At moments it felt to him like defusing a bomb, or what he imagined defusing a bomb would be like.

Indeed it was the military aspect that intrigued him. That's what he had spied in the coding: the necessary safeguards. They sat alongside the main coding components as a separate set of parameters and commands. They had not been fully integrated, not yet woven into the whole.

The machine conducted two main scans, the first was meant to analyse for and differentiate between organic and inorganic matter, and if it detected any items that could constitute weaponry of any sort then the process was automatically halted and could not be bypassed. If, however, it got through this initial test then a secondary scan was conducted, one that regarded the object being sent in a purely holistic manner. It was this second scan that was used for transmission. Information pertaining to the first was summarily discarded.

¶

'This being the fault you had identified? Perhaps you should have mentioned this at your trial.'

'Hmm. No. I was advised not to. I was told it might damage my case if I tried to undermine the network. And, yes, I suppose that does make sense.'

Items from each dish had been extracted and heaped in a single bowl. The boy blew on the food as he stirred it. He ate slowly.

'The prosecution would have attacked whatever I said. All that legal trickery: twisting my words, trying to get me into a corner, tripping me up. It wouldn't be about the truth, no, just in trying to make me look stupid or reckless or, hmm, uncaring? It'd be a show to make the public believe the network was still perfectly safe. After all, what could a scrawny kid like me know about, well, anything! Hmm, no, if they wanted a battle they weren't getting one from me. Much better to stay quiet, as advised.'

¶

Despite the flaw, the system itself impressed him immensely, now that he'd got a good look at it. But he knew it could be made better. He knew that he could himself make it better. He could simplify it, make it safer. And if he did it right, if he impressed them, they might even offer him a job. None of that routine application nonsense. No. He would demonstrate his skills directly.

The theory was simple. The units were all, by necessity, two-way. Every machine was connected to every other machine, however remotely. The coding was not fixed in a centralised location, it was a fundamental part of every individual unit. This ensured that if there was, say, a power cut in one place, then everything could still function as normal in every other place. It was meant to be beneficial, to avoid a full-on system collapse. And it worked. But it could also be exploited, if one knew how.

The boy's plan would be to send a brief interruption to the signal. It would infect all units, but only for as long as he allowed it to. It wouldn't be anything new, he would merely integrate those aspects of the code he had already identified. It was easy to do. No one would be hurt. At worst his actions would be seen as an annoyance, as a sort of prank.

Ten seconds. That was all he needed. He put through his prompt, his suggestion to the coding, for a mere ten seconds. Then he allowed the system to go back to its previous state. After which he unplugged his computer from the network and carefully eased the whole unit back into its housing.

He turned the radio on and waited.

¶

'People get so uppity about nudity, don't you think? I find that strange. We accept it without question once it has been normalised, when it's a hospital ward, or a public changing room, or when it's in our own home, yes, our own warm nest. Even when it used to be a part of travelling. People were fine with it then too. It was procedural. And yet, hmm, when it comes as a surprise, well, then everyone goes a bit—'

The boy stopped eating for a moment, his bowl in one hand lifted to the level of his chin, a white plastic fork in the other, poised, unloaded.

'My understanding—' The man dressed all in black had come forward from his dim corner. He stood now on the other side of the table, his heavy head tilted forward. '—is that nudity was not in this instance the problem.'

The boy had not seen the man change position. At the room's middle those black clothes seemed even more at odds with the harsh electric light. More than that it seemed as though the man had carried some of the dimness with him from the room's corner.

The boy blinked hard and shook his head, resuming his meal.

'Hmm, not the problem. No.' He took a mouthful and chewed it slowly, ponderously. 'But it was the intention. Yes. And the outcome too. In a way.'

'You meant no ill by it.' The man straightened. There was a long dull creak from deep within his clothes. 'It was an easy mistake to make.'

'Except there wasn't any mistake. No. Not at all. It worked exactly as I'd anticipated. It's just that I, hmm, I hadn't considered all that that might imply. In practice, I mean.'

¶

The boy sat listening to the radio but nothing unusual happened; no disruptions to the schedule, no special announcement. He listened to the news as it came on the hour but nothing out of the ordinary was reported: the usual bickering politics, the sporting results, the forecast for the days ahead.

He was certain his code-switch had worked. There was no logical reason why it shouldn't. Any transporter unit using the network within that ten-second window would have run its program differently than before. First there would have been the full scan, then the scan to differentiate between organic and inorganic matter, and then, so long as the safety checks were passed, and the boy had made sure not to tamper with those, it was this second separational scan that would be used for transmission, not the whole-object scan, and with one further twist: only organic matter would be sent. Any clothes or other accoutrements would be left in a heap on the floor of the sending chamber.

Nothing would be broken. It could all be sent on afterwards once the code had been reverted. A simple follow-on command would work just fine once the receiving chamber was clear of its naked occupant. There would be embarrassment, perhaps anger, confusion mostly, but nothing more than that. And the effects would be worldwide. Surely such a happening would be newsworthy.

But the bulletin made no such mention.

The boy turned off the radio. He sat in the kitchen and pondered on what had gone wrong. And something was indeed wrong. Something had changed. He could feel it.

It took him a while to realise the growing level of noise about him, a general sense of the air pressure increasing, a thickening of soundwaves, of sirens, of wailings, of booted feet.

He was about to look out the window when there came a sudden hammering at his front door, and with it the sound of serious voices.

¶

'It really was very strange. Yes. When they took me out-side, I mean.' The boy lifted one of the foil trays and tipped it near vertical, scooping out its contents into his bowl. 'Though, of course, they came inside first. Yes. I let them. And then there was a rush. Not at me. No. They went straight on past. They went to the machine itself. Hmm, like it was something that had been abused, something they needed to rescue. They crouched down beside it. They seemed to stroke it. They checked it for bruises. That's right. They didn't really consider me to begin with. No. I was nothing but a boy. A nobody. But then, well, hmm, when no one else was found in our house, so they turned, in a sort of slow bewilderment, upon me. In a daze they handcuffed me and led me out. And there, on the streets, there were people, walking. Yes. It was all so odd. And noisy. I'd never thought of the quietness of streets as being anything unusual, till I saw people out walking them. And these people, they too were in a daze. Like they were uncertain about this walking. Like it was a new thing. Yes. Like they weren't quite sure how walking worked. You could see it in their faces, their movements. They hadn't considered just how far away things really were. The world was just too huge. And yet they couldn't have known. Not what I'd done. No. Not all of them. It couldn't have affected so many.'

'The whole system had to be shut down. After your transmission. Everything was on hold. You stopped the world. Like that. And those people, those sorry souls, they had no choice. The full reality of the world was thrust upon them.'

'And you heard about it too? You were affected?'

The man remained silent for a while. He swayed gently. He was very tall.

'I heard. Yes. And no, I was not affected. But I knew of people who were. I knew of many people.'

¶

It took them an age to get to the police station. Too many people wandering down the middle of the road. And the officers in the police car were quiet. They seemed curiously calm. They didn't explain anything to the boy on the back seat. Every so often one would turn around and gaze at him blankly. A look that might have been uncertainty, or suppressed anger, or pity. The boy couldn't be sure.

And when at last they sat him down, and brought him tea, and read out the charges, when they told him what had happened, it was his turn to be quiet and contemplative, for him to be uncertain of his feelings.

Because it had worked. His practical experiment had worked perfectly. In that tiny ten-second window anyone using the network, across the whole world, had been affected. Only the organic part of them had been sent down the wires. Anything else had been left behind in an untidy heap.

For most this was harmless. Industry had suffered only in that a lot of raw materials had refused to send. They couldn't account for it, and before they could find out the reason, the network was shut off.

For many others they arrived, as the boy had intended, naked. And there was embarrassment and rage and borrowed blankets and asking how they could retrieve their belongings. And then there were those who came through without their crutches, or their wheelchairs, or prosthetic limbs. These individuals were found on the floor of the receiving chambers, unable to get out. And some lost their spectacles, and some lost false teeth, and some lost hearing aids. And some lost pins that were holding bones in place. And some lost pacemakers. And some lost artificial heart valves.

Even in that ten-second window, when scaled up to the entire world, to the millions of daily users, it amounted to a lot of people. There were no precise numbers available. Not everyone could be accounted for. The full effects were ongoing. They were long-lasting. Reports kept coming in.

Even when the system was deemed safe, with the culprit having been found and questioned and no further threat being posed, people didn't trust going through the network. Not at first.

All the major industries wanted special assurances that nothing would go wrong with their shipments. What had so easily come apart could not so easily be put back together again. The lost-luggage departments of the major ports were in chaos. The whole world was in chaos. And there was no back-up. There were no ships running. No aircraft. No trains. People didn't know how to get to work, or take their children to school, or do the weekly shop.

¶

'But do you know what I was thinking?' The boy looked up. He gave a sad smile. 'While they were telling me all this? I couldn't help thinking how impressive it all was. How much power the transport system had.'

'It is used the world over. It is relied upon.'

'No. Not like that. I mean that there were no news reports. Not one. There should have been. Right then and there. And of course there were later, in the days after, but right then and there they actually suppressed the news. Yes. They stopped it. They had that power, in that moment, to silence everyone, all the papers and TV and that, from talking about it. For fear, I suppose. Fear it might damage their reputation.'

'There was a lot of fear. In the air. In the people. There was a great deal of fear.'

'No. Not that. Hmm, I didn't mean all the social un- rest. I mean they did it for themselves. And all those television studios and newspaper companies and radio stations, they all agreed. Yes. Like that. Right away. They all played along. And I couldn't help thinking about *that* particular aspect, and not about, well—'

'Perhaps you too were suppressing something.'

'Hmm, perhaps. I don't think so though. No. I think I just—didn't really care so much. About all the people.'

'An understandable response.'

¶

Of course the boy became the scapegoat. He was, after all, the perpetrator. Everything, all this chaos, could rightly be laid upon his shoulders, and the boy fully accepted his culpability. No leeway was given. Nothing was played down. The crime was just too serious. Too much in the world depended upon the verdict.

It was suggested the boy had planned the disruption for months, perhaps even years. It was suggested he had dreamed of nothing else, that he had given up everything to crack the code, had been driven mad by it, till he could only see in numbers. It was suggested he had long ago lost his humanity.

His parents, too, denounced him. They said he had grown disagreeable, that he had become unruly, that he was not the son they'd once loved.

The fabrication was thorough. Everyone seemed to be in on it: old friends, former teachers, members of his extended family. It was in his best interest. It was in the world's best interest.

Of course they'd all been leaned on. It was necessary. The boy could appreciate this. And so, when he was himself spoken to, these people were not angry with him. When anyone came to visit they did not do so with any malice. They looked upon him with pity, with kindness. They were open with him. They assured him it would all be okay. They told him they had to say those things. That it was the right approach to take. That he, too, was doing the right thing.

¶

'And, you know, I think I figured it out. I realised very quickly what had gone wrong. Hmm, you see, I looked ahead, so far ahead that I could see the future. I could see what a better world it would be with the improvements I could add to the network. So, yes, I looked into that code and I understood it, like no one else had ever understood it. I looked that far forward.

By myself. It's true. And yet, hmm, I didn't quite look far enough.'

There was a rich dessert in one of the foil trays. Its hot sauce was light and fluffy, whipped to perfection so that even now when the boy came to it it had not separated.

'I was pleased with myself. Yes. Pleased with what I could see that no one else could see. But I stopped there. I didn't even think to consider beyond what I had already decided. No. I did not look far enough. I sat back, pleased with what I had done, with what I would do. And you know, when I figured this out, when I saw my own fault, I realised too that this was unacceptable. Yes. That such lazy thinking was, hmm, well, that it was beneath me. That I could have done better. But I failed. Yes. At the end of the day, I failed myself.'

He sat perfectly still for a moment, then slowly brought the spoon to his lips.

The man loomed forward over the table and stared at the boy. He stared for a long time through those impenetrably dark glasses. The boy ignored him.

'Some might say—' The man straightened. '—that you are merely a child.'

'Oh—' The boy laughed at this. 'I am. It's true. Can't ever change that. Just like everyone else, though, no? We are all the child of someone, after all. Always will be the child of someone.'

He smiled broadly at the man. The man did not smile back.

'Hmm, yes, well, perhaps the biggest mistake we all make is in thinking there's a point where we stop being children.' The boy took another hot mouthful and vaguely wagged his spoon in the air. 'Isn't that right?

Don't we fool ourselves into thinking we're grown up? At a certain point in our lives? Having reached and, hmm, passed a certain number? Regardless of how we think or what we've done. Isn't that what we're all led to believe? And that because we're older we must, well, somehow know better?'

¶

He was drugged for his trial. It was a precaution. He'd been acquiescent, even helpful, up to that point but the trial was to be televised, broadcast on all channels. They could not risk him suddenly changing his mind and using such a platform for his own ends. They said it was a mild sedation. They said it was to calm him.

He couldn't recall much of the court case itself, but afterwards he wondered that no one else had noticed. Surely everyone could see that he was quieter, slower. But no one spoke up. No one even commented. Everything was set and aiming in a single direction. It was to be the ultimate trial and the ultimate penalty. It was a necessity. It was to be a deterrent to others. It would be shown to the world that no matter how clever the criminal, such crimes would be uncovered. The culprit would be found out. They would be punished.

¶

'So, yes, I went along with it. This, hmm, this ruse. Because that's what it was, no? But I understood that. I really did. It was all for the publicity of the thing. So I played my part. And of course, yes, they never actually spoke of it. Their plan. That made sense too. I could see they'd be worried how, if I knew too much, I might not take things seriously, might even, hmm, might even play the fool. But I did know, and I did take things seriously. And I hope, yes, I hope they were aware of that. I hope they noticed.'

He glanced up at the tiny black holes in the ceiling. He smiled.

'Because it was all just a machine. Just a process. And I was just one person. One silly person who'd made a terrible mistake. Yes. But I needed to go through that machine. Right through. I needed to let it run its course and I would come out the other end and there would be my parents, my friends, my teachers, my extended family members. They'd all be there waiting for me. And not just that, I'd have a job at the institute too. Yes. Because, you know, they could surely use a mind like mine. They really could. And it's a much better mind now. Yes. Because I've made my mistake. I've seen what not to do. So, hmm, really the lesson's been learned.'

'And has anything changed your mind since?'

The boy did not answer.

¶

He had been open and engaging when they came to question him. He explained in great detail how his code had worked. He spoke directly to programmers, a small team, crammed awkwardly into his cell. They listened attentively. They noted everything down. They understood him. They were impressed. But they wanted to take it further.

This ability to separate matter into its constituent parts, it intrigued them. It was something they'd been looking into for a long time, but they couldn't quite fathom it. They felt it could have a very useful function when it came to industrial waste-disposal. A wholly new network of cables and large chambers would be set up to cater to this effect. The application itself might be rather crude, but it would solve a lot of world problems involving harmful chemicals and non-recyclables. And they would of course be very careful to keep this new system separate from the main transporter network.

But the boy could not help in this regard. What they were asking for was, he told them, impossible. Still they came often to question him. He talked and they listened. They made many notes.

And then, eventually, they stopped coming.

¶

'Did you ever wonder why they gave up?'

The man had shifted to stand behind the boy, swaying above him. The boy did not make any effort to look round as the two of them spoke. He heard the voice clearly enough. He knew the man to be there.

'Oh, no. Not really. I didn't need to wonder.'

That deep slow creaking again, as of huge trees rocked by heavy winds, sounding both close and distant all at once. The boy ignored it.

'I knew that what I was saying had finally got through to them. You see, a separation of specific identifiable materials is one thing. Yes. That's doable. But they wanted to stop the reassembly process. Like that. So I told them, no, it can't be done. It defies all logic. The information within a closed system is always retained. It has to be somewhere. Like everything else. It all has to balance out. Yes. No. You can't have a positive without a negative. You cannot have up without down. Debit and credit. Profit and loss. It's how things are. It's how they have to be.'

'You still believe this?'

'Oh, hmm, yes. I know what you're getting at. I've heard the rumours. That they managed it. That they built their new machine. Their perfect disposal system. But I don't believe that. No. Not how they meant it. Things have to go somewhere. Yes. You can't simply disappear a thing from all existence.'

'There are many who would agree with you.'

¶

There was no special ceremony. When he was taken from his cell and walked down to the chamber there was no one else about. It was no different from switching rooms. A slow transportation. He'd done it plenty of times. This chamber, however, was new.

The general nature of the device was familiar to him, but here it had been refined. An updated model. Instead of being lined with the usual misty grey bulbs everything was now a pure bright white. The boy looked hard at the walls of his new enclosure. He could see that the bulbs were all still there, but they were of a much finer grade, and they were integrated, like skin cells. He could imagine such a system being fitted up in any room without much effort, as easy as applying wallpaper.

And yet this chamber was no quick job. It had been specially designed. It had a permanence to it. And the boy stood in the very middle, with the clean white walls all around him, and he was content. He was calm. He was curious to see just what might happen next.

The sound when it began was familiar, albeit diminished, as though far away, or muffled by thick cloth. At moments it sounded like distant maintenance, like thumping and hammering from somewhere else in the building. At other moments it sounded like a deep soft gurgling and groaning, as from old creaking pipes.

There was only one thing that was niggling at the back of the boy's mind, some small detail that wasn't quite right. Something was missing. Some crucial component. He could feel its lack but couldn't quite work out what it was or what such an absence would imply. It was difficult, after all, to look for something that wasn't there.

So he tried very hard to think more. To out-think his own ability. To think beyond himself. Not to let his mind be lazy. The answer had to be attainable. The answer must exist.

But it was no good.

¶

In the cell the boy's white bowl and foil trays all sat empty. The plastic fork and spoon were spotless. Every crumb of the meal had gone. The juices mopped up, the sauce licked clean from the dish.

After a while someone came into the cell, and stacked the remaining items, and took them away.

8. Home Help

THE MOUTH of the new tunnel loomed far quicker than she had anticipated. There were red lights, there were green lights, and Anna had barely a moment to position herself correctly before she was engulfed. The icy brightness of the day was gone. A lifeless yellow pulsing took its place.

Anna calmed herself with the thought that it didn't really matter what lane she was in or how fast she was going; there was no one but her on the road. She wound her window down and listened to the lonely reverberations her engine made on the curved grey walls.

The tunnel was only new from her perspective. It would always remain so. When she was young there was a lot of talk about the benefits of having one, and the unnecessariness of having one, and the costliness of having one, and then came the many years of quiet planning during which there still wasn't one. She had moved away from the area long before any actual building work began.

Anna came out the other end of the tunnel and the day sprang back into existence. She slowed suddenly. The turning should be soon but this part of the trip always confused her. The new slip roads and signs and roundabouts didn't match with the spaces she'd known in childhood. Side roads had been neatly dead-ended. Embankments had been levelled and pavements cropped. There were fewer pylons now and their cables were slack. Around here was where the new world had been crudely bolted onto the old.

Anna dropped into low gear. The gearbox graunched; the synchromesh was shot. She winced, hissing through her teeth: that was going to be expensive. She was still going too fast as she took the unfamiliar roundabout, the long steel pipes in the back of her truck clanging loudly in protest. She tensed, slowing to a crawl. No one, after all, was pressing her to get there any quicker than she needed.

And then, all at once, Anna knew just where she was. All the lines and dimensions, the trees, the whole space of her environment, in an instant it all made sense to her again.

It never ceased to amaze her that there were still some corners of the country that weren't networked into the transmat system. Stubborn little communities still content to live off-grid. Yet she also felt a tinge of pride that one of them was the very village she'd grown up in. She hoped they might stay stubborn for a good while longer. And that strange rush of familiarity as she now drove her pick-up down the old roads that marked the area's outskirts, it wasn't mere nostalgia, it was delight in the capacity of her own mind to feel so at ease in a place from which she had long ago divorced herself.

Her truck bumped and rumbled over the cracked road. Untrimmed top-heavy hedgerows protruded over narrow pavement. She passed a car parked close into the kerb. And now a car passed her. Where could they be going? Anna checked her rearview but the car was gone, disappeared, just as she'd once disappeared.

And yet: here she was again, as easy as that, driving straight into the past, shrinking herself back into her childhood. Or no, perhaps not quite that. It was more like invading her childhood, but with the air of a knowing adult who sees things the child never noticed, never appreciated. Because now it was she who was the sophisticated out-of-towner. She'd grown up and moved on, as the world had moved on. No one would recognise her returning. No one would care.

Anna glanced at the little petrol station as she turned onto the high street. A pokey place, but part of the community nonetheless. She noted the price of fuel. Another wince. She was on the verge of shaking her head in dismay, but she caught herself and stopped. No, she mustn't think like that. The locals wouldn't think like that. They'd go about their business quite happily, and they wouldn't mind the high prices, just as they wouldn't begrudge her arrival.

Many more cars now lined the kerbs, bottlenecking the street. She had to slow to a stop to let other road-users pass by. There were people walking. She could actually see people strolling between the shops, as though it was nothing, as though it was normal. She had a momentary surge of fear that someone might wander carelessly into the road and she'd knock them down. But no, of course not, not here; she was still thinking like an out-of-towner.

A few more turnings and there was her father's house, her childhood home. One stout telegraph pole on the street corner, an octopodal splay of wires leading off in all directions, but seemingly no new additions. This she only noticed because she was looking out for it.

A comforting sight. And when she parked in front of the house it felt as though her pick-up filled the whole driveway. She felt bigger in herself as she stepped out. She had a strength, a sense of her own maturity, of her superiority. She felt somehow responsible. She had her own front-door key.

She hoisted the bag of groceries she'd brought and headed inside. This was her gift from the big city. All non-perishables. Never an easy task. Most things were fresh these days, simply because they could be. Anything was available because everything was available. But the old-fashioned tastes of the elderly were still catered for, to some extent, for the time being.

Closing the door behind her with her foot Anna stood for a moment in the dimness of the front hall, smiling at the familiar fusty airs. The same worn green carpet. The same ugly pictures. The same dark-striped wallpaper.

'Have you got it? Did you find any?'

Her father hobbled towards her out of the gloom, two short sticks extending spiderlike from his hands.

Startled to see her father advancing in such a manner Anna held open the carrier bag before her, revealing the dull glint of its contents. Her father halted to examine the offering, then gave one of his sticks to his daughter and took the bag from her, clutching it to his chest as he lurched away towards the kitchen.

'And are you going to tell me what's happened?' Anna followed him. '—what you've done to yourself this time?'

'What? Nothing.' He gave a little grunt as he lifted the carrier bag high and let it thump down on the sideboard. 'A fall. That's all. Why does everybody insist on fussing so?' He began extracting the tins one at a time. Some were anchovy fillets; some were lychees in thin syrup; most were corned beef. He arranged the tins in front of him, working one-handed, muttering as he did so. 'Ridiculous why you can't get them in the village. *Oh, no, sorry, we don't stock them*, they say. *Nobody likes them*, they say. Utter nonsense. I know half a dozen hereabouts who'd buy them. Regularly, too. *No, it's not that*, they say, *they're just too expensive for us to bring in*. Well, I hope you won the battle there. Got them at a good price and all.' He stopped and turned to his daughter. 'Well?'

'Hmm?'

'How much do I owe you?'

'What? Oh—nothing. It doesn't matter. I know of a place.'

She didn't like to say that the only way to get them was from abroad, via the network. Only a handful of small countries still produced them; a hangover from previous generations when such things were considered delicacies. Ordering them in wasn't difficult, but they weren't exactly cheap. More than this, however, Anna felt her father would only complain they tasted wrong if he knew just how they'd been acquired.

'Good girl. Beating the system. That's what I like to hear. Maybe get some more next time though. These won't last very long if I have guests. Tea?'

'Dad, what fall? Why don't I know about this?'

Her father, with great effort, filled the kettle and switched it on. 'I suppose you'll want biscuits or something. They're in the larder. Big round tin. Top shelf. You know where.'

Anna fetched the biscuits as directed. And yes, she knew where. She still had to stretch to get them, but that was an improvement over having to balance on tiptoes on a wobbly stool.

When she re-emerged her father was already seated by the window, well away from the now hissing kettle. Anna began setting a tray.

'The fall, Dad. You're supposed to notify me.'

'Except I was in hospital.'

'Which is exactly why I need to know.'

'Which is exactly why I couldn't tell you.'

'Because I'd worry?'

'No, because I was in hospital. Think, girl. I couldn't get to a phone.'

Anna took a deep breath and held it. She clenched her jaw. She focused on making the tea.

She'd found herself considering his vulnerability more and more in recent years, but now there would be a new worry: if something serious did happen, she wouldn't even know. No one would tell her. She'd arrive one day with a whole pallet of corned beef, but he'd be gone.

And it was pointless arguing. He'd somehow turn her worry into a sign she was being selfish, that her own supposed feelings mattered more than his actual well-being, or of his being at all.

Anna sat down at the table's opposite end. The tray was placed between them.

'And how long have you been back?'

'From the ward? Oh, a few weeks or so.' He waved a biscuit dismissively.

Anna raised her eyebrows. Her father didn't notice.

'It's all worked out rather well, actually. The council

have it all in hand, you see. They've visited several times already. They're going to rig up some sort of, uh, system for me. One of those—you know, transport whatchamacallits. Yes. Make me more mobile. More independent. Safer too. Any problems and—*shoom*—just like that, straight into hospital. No phone calls. No fuss.'

'What?' Anna stared wide-eyed at her father, a biscuit poised at her open mouth. 'But they can't.' She lowered the biscuit back to her plate. 'And you hate that system. Like, really hate it. You said you'd never use it. Never. And they—they just can't.'

'But they can, and I don't, and I did, and—they will.'

'But it'd be far too expensive. They'd have to dig up the garden. They'd dig up the roads for sure. There would be new pylons everywhere. Huge ugly things. No one here would agree to it. And you—you certainly can't afford any of that.'

Anna's father smiled and shook his head. 'I don't have to. Government scheme, you see? Our council, or rather our *area*, as they called it, has been selected. It'll be free. Totally free. And not just me, the whole village. Just a few houses at first, yes, probably. That's only sensible. But it'll soon spread.'

'Even for a few houses that's still a lot of infrastructure they'd need. For the cabling alone. It'll take months to install all that. And you'd hate it. The noise. The mess. Dad, please, if you're genuinely worried about your mobility I could—rig something up for you myself. I could design it. Build it. No trouble. Something to get you upstairs. If need be I could even come and stay here. I don't mind. It wouldn't—'

Her father shook his head again and took from his pocket a well-creased pamphlet. He smoothed it and slid it forward over the table.

Anna glanced at it briefly.

'No.' She looked back at her father. 'No, Dad. Not this.'

'No cables, you see. Not any more. This here—' He poked at the pamphlet. 'This is the future. Things are moving on!'

'Dad, this is—not a good idea. It really isn't.' Anna gingerly unfolded the pamphlet. 'You know what this is, don't you?'

'Oh yes. I know exactly. They've explained it to me. To everyone. It's really very straightforward.'

'No, Dad. It's not straightforward at all. It's very un-straightforward. And unsafe. And untested.'

'Oh, but it will be. That's us, you see? We're to be those test subjects. That's why it's all for free.'

'Exactly! Can't you see that's why you should say no? You can't let them use you like that. Because when it all goes wrong—'

'Don't be so melodramatic. Of course it won't go wrong. They wouldn't be spending all this money on it if it didn't already work.'

'But this is just a dream. A fantasy.' Anna raised the pamphlet. She flapped it accusingly. 'It's not actually real. And even if it is theoretically possible it's still decades away from being practicable. You don't even know how the system works right now. You never did. You never accepted that such a thing could ever work, despite the evidence. And now you're suddenly ready to accept this? This?'

Her father's face remained passive. When he spoke his voice was calm and assured. The same manner and tone he'd employed when Anna was young.

'The practicability, dear girl, is quite simple. It's merely a matter of finding a route. A tunnel. It's no different from using a cable. The cabled system provides a fixed route, a clear route. The new system needs only to find a route through air. A sure path. Just as lightning finds its sure path to the earth—'

At this Anna flipped open the pamphlet again. She'd noticed a picture of lightning on her first glance inside. And yes, there was the passage underneath, near word for word what her father was now spouting.

'—And so, when lightning arcs from the clouds it needs to create its own route in the very moment of its making. It puts out feelers, it forks, it tests the air, looking for that sure path, that clear hole through the ether. And when at length one of those bright tendrils touches the earth, then, and only then—it strikes. It downloads its full charge. All that energy, zapped, in an instant, surely and precisely, down through nothing but air, right into the ground.'

Anna's father stopped. He sat looking at his daughter. He wore a contented smile.

Anna sniffed and shook her head. 'Feelers? Ether? Bright tendrils?' She tossed the pamphlet back onto the table. 'You know what they're doing, don't you? Filling you with all that nonsense? Just because they say it works, doesn't mean it's true.'

'Of course it works. It is a natural physical phenomenon. It just happens so fast we don't observe it. Indeed it happens at the very speed of—'

'Yes, yes, the speed of light. I know. I've read what it says. But it doesn't mean that's how this—this cableless system really would work.'

'But how else could—'

'It's just an image! Nothing more. A model. Something to put in your head. Something to convince you. Which is exactly what it has done. Clearly.'

Anna's father shrugged. 'Then how do you think it does work?'

'What? I—how should I know?'

'But you cannot deny that it must, or else they wouldn't be installing it. They wouldn't be going to all this bother. All this, as you so rightly say, expense.'

'No.' Anna's voice dropped. She clicked her thumbnail against her teeth. 'I don't know.' She leaned forward suddenly. 'But that's not the point! What matters is that you don't even need it! You never did before and you don't now. It's not necessary. And where would you go anyway? To the hospital? Is it really worth it just for that? Or for the convenience of going to the shops and back? Really? And only then if they're connected, anyhow, because if they're not then what *is* the point?'

'Oh, Anna.' Her father looked at her sorrowfully. 'I really thought you'd understand. You of all people. This system doesn't need connectors. It's connector-free. It just needs a transceiver dish. And then the dish is aligned to the nearest mast. Nothing more to it. So simple. That there is your clear path. Your sure route. It hops between masts. It's not random. And, what's more, it's not just for long distance. You know what you were saying about getting up the stairs? Well, just you take a look at this.'

Another partly-crumpled pamphlet was extracted from the folds of her father's cardigan and pushed over the table.

This one was not as glossy; printed simply, in green ink on plain white paper. Anna did not pick it up. She didn't have to. Her father carried on talking regardless.

'Fully-integrated internal transfer. Room to room. It comes with a hand-held controller. You press a button and—*pop*—you're upstairs. In an instant. Or in the bathroom. Or out in the garden. Or—oh, no, wait— maybe not the garden. I'll have to check that. I'm not sure that's covered.'

Frowning he slid the pamphlet back towards himself and leaned in to pore over it.

Anna sighed. Open transfer. Cableless. Holes through the air. Roof-mounted dishes. It was all too much.

'Dad, please. Just wait. That's all I ask. Just—wait. Don't let yourself be a test subject. Wait till it's all been standardised. Wait till they've ironed out all the glitches. Because—because something will be up with it. There'll be something they've not thought of. Something they'll need to correct. And in the meantime I could put up—I don't know, a set of rails. A wheeled trolley that can get you from room to room. You'd like that. And I'd like building it for you. Or perhaps we could simply—reorder the house. Make it so you don't even need to get upstairs. So that you won't ever—'

'No.' Anna's father looked up sharply from the pamphlet. The corners of his mouth downturned. 'Not out into the garden. Not yet at any rate. That's a pity. I would've liked that. Much faster getting inside if it started to rain.'

Anna's throat had gone dry. She wanted to speak but all that came out was air. She coughed. Her father looked momentarily concerned. Then he smiled.

'It's alright, old girl. I'll be alright. I won't have to worry about a thing, and neither will you. Surely that's better all round. And they'll maintain it too. For free. All part of the service. All part of the trial. Plus you'll be able to visit more easily. Or I could visit you, eventually. Probably.' He frowned for a moment, then brightened. 'Time for something new, eh? Time to—embrace change. And what with your mother gone it'll be so much—'

'She'd never have agreed to it.'

'Oh, well, maybe so, but she'd soon—' Anna's father stopped. He looked away. He gazed out the window into the small but busy garden. 'No. Quite right. She'd have protested. And in the very same way you're protesting.' He breathed in. 'But she's not here, dear thing, and I—well.'

Anna didn't press her father to continue. The discussion, for the time being, was over.

That night she slept in her old room, in her old bed. She didn't sleep easy. She rarely did when staying over. She found it hard to relax in a space once considered her own that had long ago been cleaned and simplified, redecorated with soft floral wallpaper and darkwood furnishings, converting it into a bland and tidy guest room.

Anna did not feel much like a guest. There was a lot more to her these days beyond being bigger and better-travelled, but she was still her father's child. She knew there was little she could do to stop him in his new venture. His mind was made up—or had been made up for him.

But he had never been rash with his decisions. No doubt he would have taken a lot of convincing. Most of all he would have needed to convince himself, after which it would be impossible to turn him back.

Anna tried to tell herself that it was all somehow for the best. She tried to imagine all the benefits: how her father would be more mobile, independent, and how eventually this new system would become standard in any case; it would become the norm. If he didn't accept their offer of free installation now then the world would simply move on without him, again—so long as he was still around.

Anna tensed her jaw, trying to push the thought away. A small radio stood on the bedside table. She put it on low and turned over.

¶

On her next trip to see her father Anna found as she approached the village that the oncoming lanes of the tunnel had been closed off. There were no roadworkers to be seen, just signs and barricades. The tunnel itself looked as new as ever. All the lights were on, curving away into the concrete interior. Traffic had been rerouted along Anna's side of the road, splitting the carriageway. It didn't make any difference: Anna's truck was the traffic. All of it. She'd not seen a single vehicle coming the other way all morning. At least in this direction she didn't need to make a lane adjustment. She had only to keep on going.

Anna found her father in the living room. He was sitting, very still, in a large armchair, his arms out to either side, head back, eyes closed, mouth open. He was wearing what looked like an all-in-one set of disposable overalls, such as might be worn for painting the walls. The overalls were pale blue. They had a faint pearlescent sheen.

There was music playing. Opera of some sort. Anna didn't recognise it. She didn't much like opera. The hi-fi cabinet had its doors wide and on the floor were two dusty wooden boxes full of old records. The music was loud. It filled all the air of the small room. Anna knew better than to disturb her father while it played. He wouldn't have heard her come in.

She seated herself amid the mess that covered the sofa: a skewed stack of pictures in their frames, a variety of shelf ornaments. She sat leaning forward, her knees together. The carrier bag she'd brought with her she lowered carefully to rest between her feet, its heavy contents settling.

The room was in disarray, as was the hallway she'd come through and the kitchen she'd peeked into. At a glance it looked as though the whole house was being redecorated, the walls all stripped, ready for new paper to be put up. But when Anna looked more carefully she could see that the old wallpaper was still there, except it had been patched over now with huge white sheets of woodchip. No, not woodchip. The pattern was too regular for woodchip. And the sheets had that same faint pearlescent quality to them. They looked more like bubblewrap than anything, but the bubbles were very fine, and packed together closely, without gaps.

These sheets were crudely hung. They weren't pasted, they'd been stapled in place. There were creases at their edges where each black staple pinned them to the walls. And not only the walls, they covered the ceiling too. The whole set-up looked rather ugly. It looked like shoddy workmanship.

The music rose to its last cadence, and stopped. Anna's father came to life. His eyes opened and he sat forward. He squinted briefly at his daughter and glanced up at the ceiling, before easing himself from his chair and stepping over to the boxes of records. His movements were assured, even sprightly. There was no sign of him hobbling any more.

'Now, wasn't that magnificent?' He took the record from the player and sleeved it.

Anna sat expressionless. 'I don't think any music could cover up for how horrible this room looks—or feels.'

'You know—' Her father's fingers paused upon the stack of LPs. 'I've not heard any of these for years. They were in the top room. Only found them yesterday. I was worried the mould might have got to them, but no, they still play alright.'

'If you're taking requests, how about a concerto.'

Anna's father grimaced. 'Horrible virtuosic nonsense. All show. No real substance.' He fingered idly through the stack.

'And opera isn't? With those wailing arias? After all, if you're wanting to tell a good story, opera is hardly the best way to do it.'

'Ah!' Her father pulled out a disc with a hopeful expression. 'Will a quintet suffice as a compromise?'

Anna smiled. 'Sure. Quintets are okay.'

A brief moment of accord. The music was set going but with the volume lowered. Anna's father stood with a satisfied look and put his hands on his hips to stretch his back, grunting as he did so.

Anna could see now that whatever her father was wearing it was not a set of disposable overalls. The loose-fitting fabric was thicker. It had a coarse weave. It covered his feet like a baby's romper suit. A hood flopped at his shoulders. Anna took a breath.

'This is it. Isn't it. This is that new system.' Anna gestured vaguely at the walls. She wrinkled her nose. 'Not exactly very pretty. I'd have expected it to be a lot slicker.'

'It's just a preliminary set-up. For calibration. To get a sense of the space.' He continued his stretches.

'I hope they'll neaten it up eventually.'

Narrow strips of wiring poked from the base of the stippled wall-sheets. They followed the skirting and carried on into the hallway.

'All that stuff's for the inner loop. The wires make it easier to zip from room to room.'

'But why would you need to? And why every room? Why not, say, an upstairs and a downstairs?'

'Well, why not? Makes it more convenient, don't you think? And then by using this—' He rummaged in the pocket of his romper suit and brought out something akin to a calculator, but longer, and with fewer buttons. '—I can choose where I want to go.'

'Of course.' Anna nodded, wincing at how easily he handled the object, worrying it might go off at any moment. 'So long as you don't lose it.'

'Not that it's working presently. No batteries. And things aren't yet linked up in any case. I'm just getting used to the feel of it.' Anna's father slumped back in his armchair. 'And then this thing.' He took a thick pinch of the coarse blue fabric and held it forward before letting it sag back. 'They call this a tracker suit.'

'You mean a tracksuit.'

'No. Tracker suit. It tracks you. Or, no—it doesn't actually do the tracking. The walls do the tracking. But you need to wear the suit so the walls can locate you.'

Anna made a face. 'You mean you have to wear that at all times?'

'It's for convenience.'

'Seems kind of crazy. And it looks uncomfortable.'

'It's much softer on the inside.'

'And what, you go through the cables wearing it too? Do they expect you to go to the shops like that?'

'Not cables, no. Cableless now, remember. But yes— if need be, I'd go to the shops like this.' He read his daughter's expression. 'Oh, you don't need to look like that. What are clothes but a convention, anyhow? And if it's what everybody else is wearing, and it likely soon will be, then what's the problem? No one will be embarrassed. We'll all look the same.'

'Sounds dull.'

'Not at all, not at all. It's exciting! And it'll help strip away those ridiculous notions of *fashion* and *glamour*. It'll be like a uniform. Utilitarian, no less. People will be happier not having to compete with one another for who looks best. It'll make people calmer. It really is rather democratic.'

Anna was too tired to argue. If he wanted to look like a fool that was up to him. But she wouldn't herself be caught wearing such an outfit. She lifted the carrier bag onto the sofa beside her, dumping it awkwardly on a pile of magazines.

Her father was already lying with his head back, listening to the music, his mouth moving as he followed the notes. He didn't seem at all interested in what his daughter had brought him from the city.

That night Anna slept more easily. Not because she was any more content with the situation, but because she was so very weary. She didn't care that her old bedroom had also been fitted with the new system, all the walls crudely covered over with the strange white bubblewrap. It was only when she set off the next morning that she felt a sense of dread. As she drove slowly out of the village she saw company vans dotted all over the place, in driveways, outside shops, in the school grounds. And there were workmen too, all wearing overalls, just like her father. Except they also wore heavy boots and hard hats. And they carried rolls of the white bubblewrap from their vans. And they climbed up on roofs to fix transceiver dishes in place. And in the middle of the village Anna saw they were erecting a huge mast, like a giant metal matchstick, its pale pinkish head towering above the houses.

¶

It was a further two months before Anna made her next visit. She had to brake hard as she rounded the corner that brought the tunnel entrance suddenly into view. Now all the lanes were closed. The whole mouth of the tunnel was loosely barricaded with cones and warning signs and flapping plastic tape.

Anna pulled to a stop but kept the engine running. The lights inside the tunnel were off. Just a dark gaping hole boring into the hillside. She tried to think back. Had she missed the diversion? Had she been so complacent with the emptiness of the roads that she hadn't paid proper attention?

She considered going through the tunnel anyway. There was no one about. She could progress carefully. It would probably all be fine.

But no, she couldn't bring herself to do it. She would have no excuse if she was found out. She bumped her truck over the central reservation and headed back the way she'd come. She had to travel several miles before she found an alternative route. Despite still being so near to her home town she didn't know this part of the countryside. She didn't like the unfamiliarity.

In the village there was hardly a parked car to be seen. The petrol station had closed down. High metal fences enclosed its barren forecourt. There was no one out on the main street of the village. It was like a ghost town. No, Anna could see lights on in some of the shops, and as she drove by at a crawl, ducking her head low, she could see signs of movement within.

At least her father's house looked the same from outside. But the sound of her cab door thocking shut seemed strange in the village's unnatural quiet. It sounded sharp, without depth, without echo, as though the noise barely travelled in the still air.

Anna convinced herself this was just her imagination. Here, after all, was the same front porch. Here was the same odd angle she had to use for her key to turn the lock smoothly. She stepped in and closed the door.

'Dad?'

Her voice, despite its loudness, died the instant it left her lips. She waited for a while. There was no answer.

The hall carpet felt strange beneath her feet. There was a sort of stuffiness around her, like no one had opened a window in there for weeks.

The radiators must have come on a moment before she arrived. She could hear them ticking and gurgling as the metals expanded and water washed through the pipes. It was only when she was in the kitchen and had laid her small carrier bag on the table that Anna noticed the pilot light on the boiler was out. And yet she could still clearly hear the system, its random knocks, its hissings and rumblings. She looked around to see if a secondary boiler had been installed. Only then did she notice once more the strange wallpaper and realised all the rooms were now done, that indeed the entire house had been fully converted.

Things had been neatened up since her last visit, so the change was not so obvious. The wiring had been tucked away, the thick black staples painted out. But if she looked hard she could still see the joins between the sheets of bubblewrap. And, now that she thought about it, the noise she could hear, the constant soft knocking, the buzz, the fine whine, it wasn't the radiators at all, and it wasn't random. The noise seemed to be more evident every time she moved.

Anna raised her arm and swung it slowly, tentatively, through the stuffy air. From behind the walls there came a rapid thrumming, a soft rattle, and then back to that high-pitched whine, all undercut by a fine mechanical itch.

Anna was being tracked. She was being analysed, continuously. With every fresh movement she made she was being assessed, and the system was recalibrating, recalculating.

'But it can't—I'm not wearing—'

She swallowed.

'Dad?'

Her voice felt very thin and wavery. The house was empty. But the house did not feel empty. The house itself was very present, and it was all around her.

Anna had had her own walk-in unit in her apartment for years. She used it regularly enough. But it never felt like this. When she was in the machine at home, she was in and prepped and ready to go, and that was that. It was no more awkward than any other sort of travelling. But this permanent readiness: the constant crackle of analysis—

Perhaps it would reject her. Perhaps, without the proper clothing, without the pale blue romper suit, it would register her presence, yes, but only as an object, not as a viable user. It would ignore her. It would regard her as mere furniture, albeit moving.

Anna scribbled a quick message on the wad of paper by the cooker. And all the while the walls were watching her, reading over her shoulder. Then soundlessly she backstepped out of the house, pulling the front door very softly shut.

Even in her own small sturdy truck Anna didn't feel at ease. She leaned out of her window to reverse from the driveway before trundling, cautiously, quietly, through the still centre of the village and back out onto the main carriageway.

The roads, as ever, were empty. But on the hills about her she could see now that new masts had been going up. Bright slender matchsticks poking into the sky, their rounded heads, nacreous and glistening, creating a network of points.

Anna wound her window up tight as she gained more speed. She didn't much like the taste of the air coming in.

9. Cut Out

'SAY AGAIN, Anji? There's too much noise. Speak into the mouthpiece. Hold it closer.'

'I said it's fine, Ma. I'm at the port. I'm—just waiting. We're all—[HISS]'

'And was it good? Did you have fun? Did the others like it? The performance?'

[INDISTINCT CHATTER—LAUGHING]

'Anji?—Hallo? I—I can't hear you properly.'

'Yeah, yeah, it was good, Ma. We're just waiting. It's taking so so long.'

'Have you got a window yet? They should have given you a time slot by now.'

'Yeah—No. It's just like really busy. Miss Anders says it's because they—[HISS]—and worse each year.'

'But come direct, okay? You'll do that? I hope you have your card. Look in your pockets. Please make sure they scan it properly. And you must must *must* double-check the address when they do. Always check it yourself.'

'It's gonna be so much easier when the—[OBSCURED BY CUSTOMER ANNOUNCEMENT]—around, really just so much better.'

'Anji?—Say again?—I didn't hear.'

'When it goes cableless, Ma. When that's all up and running it'll be—[HISS]—especially for internationals. Then you can zip right over the ocean—*pheww*—just like that. Right from your—[HISS]—and so so quick.'

'If I only knew when you'd be back, I could have your dinner ready.'

'[*HISS*]—eaten. That's one thing we—[*INAUDIBLE*]—really good here.'

'Anji? It's getting worse. What was so good?'

'[*LAUGHTER*]—Yeah—It's fine, Ma. Really. I'll tell you everything tonight.'

'Alright, but if you're very late I might be out. I'm at your aunt's from eight. Remember—from eight. Write it down.'

'Okay, Ma. It's all okay. I'll be in—'

[*SUDDEN SILENCE*]

'Hallo?—Anji?'

¶

'—no, there's been no reported delay, nothing out of the—Of course, madam. Do you have the travelcard details?—Thank you—I'm sorry but nothing's coming up on that code, do you perhaps have the—Yes, I can try a different search parameter on that if—Okay, and where was she travelling in from?—Yes, there were certainly no reported issues today. Ah no, wait, unless this is—Excuse me, sorry, may I put you on hold for a moment?—No, I'd just like to check something with my supervisor—Thank you.'

[*ELECTRONIC PIANO MUSIC*]

'Hello? Mrs Mulligan?—Yes, thank you for your patience—Yes, there's no record of that on our system for today—No, not under that name—What I mean is, I'm afraid we can't confirm such a transfer took place—No, I'm afraid that's not showing—I'm very sorry but

that information just isn't available—I'm sorry, but—
No, I'm afraid I can't see any—Mrs Mulligan?'

¶

'That's true, perhaps, of course, but they will need proof.
Honest reliable proof. I think we can be pretty sure
they're not going to take the case any further without
something solid to go on.'

'What about the teacher? She must count as a credible
witness. Didn't she say she saw the girl get into the
travel bay? Actually into it?'

'Let me see. Miss Anders, you mean? I think that's—
Yes, that's what we've got here for the *initial* report.
But when properly interviewed, when the full legal
implications had been explained to her, well, then she
couldn't be so sure. After that she said she only *thought*
she saw the Mulligan girl get in. There were so many
other pupils, you see. She couldn't monitor them all
individually.'

'What of the children themselves? The girl's friends?
Someone must have seen her go.'

'No. You'd have thought so, but no. They've all been
questioned. They're all willing to swear they went
through before her.'

'Well, in any case, we can't settle. We can't be seen to.
It's tantamount to admitting we're at fault. To admitting
that something actually happened.'

'I fully agree. And we did make an offer. A gesture. A
rather substantial one in fact. Free travel. For her and
nine others. Friends and family. A lifetime subscription
for each of them.'

'That does seem very generous. I hope she appreciates what that would amount to. In real money, I mean. How did she respond?'

'Rather curious, actually. I have it here somewhere. Yes. She asked just how long we considered a lifetime to be.'

¶

[*She is on her hands and knees on the living-room floor. She is taking apart the unit with a screwdriver. Prising off the front plate and shining her torch in before delving further. She is pulling out the innards. The sparseness surprises her. How sturdy and sculpted the unit looks on the outside, but inside it's just plastic and wiring. A couple of simple circuit boards. Some thin gold-plated contacts. Nothing to suggest its functional complexity. She takes pictures. She has two sets printed, one of which she takes to a newspaper with her story. They listen keenly. They write down all she says. They tell her they'll be in touch once they've conducted an investigation, that they'll want more from her: details of her daughter's childhood, family portraits.*]

¶

'You see, Mrs Mulligan, technically the units are still company property, even when installed in a private residence. It's illegal to tamper with them. And when the newspaper sent us your photographs, well, it was our duty to respond—'

'Where's my daughter? Where's Anji?'

'It's very clear in the original purchase documentation. We have the forms right here. We have your signature—'

'Was she still alive when you found her? Was she in pain?'

'Not only can action such as yours incur heavy fines, it's also very dangerous. For yourself, yes, and for the network as a whole—'

'What did you do with her body?'

'You have to understand, we have billions of users all over the world. Literally billions—'

'Was she sent somewhere else? Somewhere she can't get back from?'

'Statistically, it is very much the safest way to travel. You only have to look at the figures—'

'How many have gone missing?'

'It's a robust system, yes, very much so, but only in so far as it's not interfered with. And we're afraid your actions—'

'Was she surrounded by strangers? Did you comfort her?'

'On this occasion, however, due to your particular machine being a much older unit, we'd be happy to provide a replacement, a more recent model. At our expense, naturally—'

'Did she understand what was happening to her?'

'And when our new cableless system is rolled out nationwide then of course we will again provide the necessary upgrade—'

'Did she call for me? My Anji. Did she cry out?'

'Thank you, Mrs Mulligan. Be assured we'll be contacting you very soon regarding delivery and installation—'

¶

'Oh, aye, she'd be there. Standing outside Parliament. All days. All weathers. With that big floppy placard of hers. And I did feel sorry for her. Well, you would. No one else was about, see. Empty streets and that. And even if they could have seen her from the windows, if they could see altogether that far, they ignored her. Everybody did. Aye, but not me. I went and stood right beside her. Just for a bit, mind. You know, in solidarity. Well, it seemed the proper thing to do. And I agreed with her. I honestly did. In a roundabout way. I always thought something was up. You know, something a bit suspect. Something being *suppressed*, you might say. And I don't mean just with her own lass. Oh, no no no. I'm thinking a great deal wider than that. How many have been lost that we don't even hear about, eh? I mean, they *say* it's far safer than them old traditional forms of transport. But they would, wouldn't they. And I'm not even thinking of just this country. What about abroad? In them poorer places. No doubt it's all part of some government scheme. International, like. A kind of, you know, *ethnic cleansing*. That's what they call it, right? Easy way to take care of so many. To sort out all that overpopulation. A few hundred thousand at a pinch. Gone. Just like that. So, well, I put it to her. My theory. I told her I was *on her side*. I'm not sure she really heard me. She was generally very quiet. Serene, you might say. Just stood there staring at the Parliament buildings. Propping up that bloody placard. And no, to be perfectly frank, I don't think it'll make any difference. The system's far too ingrained. Nothing to be done now. But, you know, good on her, all the same. You've got to admire that kind of persistence. That resolve.'

¶

[*She is kneeling on the floor of her living room holding a large pair of scissors. Around her lie faded newspapers and fanned magazines. She is cutting out reports, essays, photographs. She places the strips and shreds into a shoebox. She doesn't read the articles. She lingers a little over the pictures: their strange suggestion of reality for something no longer present. The television is on, its volume thinned to a needly whine. A panel of commentators and academics on a dimly-lit stage in front of a studio audience.*]

'—and yet if this person ceases to exist, just like that. I mean, really gone. How can we then prove she was ever there at all? What is our evidence?'

'Or, if she has in fact become particles, and those particles can still be said, in and of themselves, to exist, is it even true to say she is *really gone*? Then again, under what rule can we say those particles qualify as being *her*?'

'By which you mean she is not *gone*, as such, merely that she's changed form? Become something else?'

'Precisely. With the *life* we knew her as having, so to speak, being only one aspect *of* that existence. And perhaps, it could then be argued, not even her *own* existence.'

'In that she was, or had been, in and of herself, merely the continuation of another's? Or some other *thing's*?'

'Indeed, and that *she* has now moved on towards something else, some other plane of existence. You see, the tendency, as ever, is for us to consider the issue only from our own limited perspective, not from that of the elemental matter itself.'

'But if what we *call* existence, if what we call *living*, beyond the existence of mere *matter*, if that *is* our existence, is, for want of a better word, *life*, then yes, I think it is fair to say, in our own terms, that she has indeed ceased to—'

'Oh, but there is no *mere* about it. We must be careful not to let our personal concerns get in the way of the underlying truths. And what, after all, qualifies any one state, one mode of being, to outrank the other? To say that *this* is life but not *that*.'

'And yet *we* are the ones talking. These are *our* words, *our* method of communication, and we, by dint of creating and using them, get to say what, if anything, those words actually mean. So, yes, if to *us*, to our *selves*, we then choose to say—'

'So what you're saying is that it's a matter of semantics? Of reducing an argument to the mere meaning of *words*? To our empirical, as opposed to our radical, understanding of the matter? To what we may impose upon a set of letters? Upon a sound? To a point of view? An *opinion*?'

'No, I believe that matters of truth still have to be, by their nature, communicable, and if you are to distort that manner of communication by taking it outside the realms of our own experience, if indeed you fail to communicate the reality of what you propose, then what, if anything, are you achieving in your—'

[*She is gazing at the screen. She watches without anger, without expression. Her cheeks feel heavy. The slow hard pulse of her heart makes her neck quiver. She turns the television off. Her fingers are trembling as she removes the batteries from*

the remote control. Like removing spent cartridges from a gun.
She places the inactive device in the cupboard under the sink.
She puts the batteries in the cutlery drawer.]

¶

'I feel for her. I really do. I know it's not the same but
I do know how she feels. I lost my watch once. And
that was my grandmother's. She gave it to me on her
deathbed. It was gold. Unique. It was the only memory
I had of her. I wore it everywhere but when I got back
from holiday it had gone. It must have been rejected by
the system. These things happen. I cried for weeks but
eventually I had to accept that I was never going to get
it back, that there was nothing to be done.'

'That's awful, sure, but it's no reason to give up. Something can always be done. Personally I say rip out all
the machines. The whole damn lot of them. Rip them
out at the roots and all their horrible wires worming
through the world. Don't use them. Just don't. It's so
simple. Never use them again. Then it can't happen. It
simply can't happen.'

'I hear you. But you know they won't. You know
they're never going to do that. It's too late to change
now. The roots go too deep. They don't just run
through the earth, they've woven their way right into
society. I agree with you. I really do. And I wish it was
so. There was a time when we didn't need it, but now
we have it, and because we have it we do need it, and
folk won't want that taken away. They wouldn't stand
for it. Everything would collapse. The whole state of
society would fall apart.'

'Would it though? I mean, really? If it were all ripped out, all the—whatever it's called, all that infrastructure? Would it really be so impossible to continue? Are we so stupid we couldn't get by?'

'Yes. I think so. I'm sorry. I don't like it any more than you, but yes. We've made the world what it is and we have to live with what we've made it. All the old trade routes are dead and rusting. We don't think about that because it's so dull, but there it is. They're forgotten. Ignored. You can't simply start them up again. Not just like that. And of course the whole world runs on trade, as we're always told. We made that of it too.'

'You know what I hate most, though? How they talk about her case being a freak statistic, a mere anomaly. A one-in-a-million chance, they say. But that's not how it is at all. One in a million? No. Not for her. For her it's one in one. You see? For her it's everything. Her girl was her everything. And she's lost. Gone forever. I wish people could understand that. I wish people could see that we aren't just a lot of numbers bumbling through life and that a few lost here and there don't matter.'

¶

'—yes, it's an important industry—yes, I accept that— no, that's not what I'm proposing—no, of course not— what I'm proposing, if you'll please let me—no, what I'm—no, that's not the case at all—yes, and all methods of travel have their dangers, this can't be ignored, just as all aspects of life have their dangers—no, it's true, and just to live is to—just to live is to—well, if you really believe such a comment to be in the public interest—

no, if I may be allowed to finish my point—it comes down to choice, yes, the choice of the individual—yes, real choice and—no, an informed choice—yes, no—it comes down to information, and if those users—if those users—if people who choose to use the system—yes, of course, everybody uses it, yes, that is the whole point—no, I believe they do have a choice—that we all—yes, even in the poorer countries—yes, we still do—no, if I may finish—if they can be informed of the inherent dangers—no, not a warning, if they can be informed of—well, I believe it is indeed a matter of education—yes, and the inherent dangers—the inherent dangers—the dangers implicit in such use—no, it is not scaremongering—the truth is that loss of life—no, the truth is—the truth is—indeed, that is the truth—and if that could be made evident—yes, an informed decision—that is exactly my point—and as such my proposal—'

¶

[*She has switched off everything, all the many devices in her home. She has turned them off at the wall, pulled out the plugs and left them dangling, and now she sits in silence, disconnected. And in that silence the hum coming from her new machine is even greater. There is no power switch on this model, no wiring she can get at. It is plumbed in. It is never off. It is never not working. And she sits by it. She leans her back against it and she listens to that hum. And she wonders what may be going round and round the network still: what might by some other freak occurrence come out of it. So long as there is still that hum. So long as there's still power going through it.*]

¶

'Okay, and next on the agenda, the closing down of the old cabled system. What are we talking about here? Months? Years?—Okay, that's not too bad, so long as all the masts are in place—Well, we need to be certain that everybody has completed their conversion—No, I really mean everybody. I don't want anyone being left out on this. Not a single soul—Well, naturally, but if we don't make that effort, if we don't make that promise, then there's gonna be complaints—Of course, and the preference is for an open system—Exactly, as opposed to a closed loop. That was always the intention—No, I think it's unwise to have them running for too long in tandem, it could cause problems in the unforeseeable. So it's best we press on as and when we—Yes, and how are things progressing with the travelsuits, with the tracker systems?—Do we have a full range of designs yet? Young and old? His and hers? Minis and maxis?— No, but I've seen preliminary sketches—Sure, I liked them—Well, yeah, from what I've seen—I agree. I think that alone could be a very profitable division. It's what people want after all. It's what they *will* want— Good, get on it right away. And get some big names involved. It shouldn't be too hard—Oh, and what of the affair with the, uh—the Mulligan woman? How did that play out—No, I didn't get round to reading the whole report. Something about, what, a power cut? Is that true? Could that really happen?—Well, I need more than best guesses here, I need—Right—I see— So what you're really saying is you've no idea—Okay, well then say so—Good—But a power cut? I mean,

I gotta say, that sounds pretty lame to me—Sure, fine, if you think that's even conceivable. But why wasn't this ever predicted? Seems fairly fundamental to the whole—You mean after transmission but before arrival? So, that's got to be like, what, nanoseconds? That's got to be speed-of-light stuff, no? And surely you're not suggesting—Well, okay, if you think it's really possible—Yes, that goes without saying. But, no matter how unlikely, I think it's still crucial we—Excuse me, it's a major concern if I say it's a major concern, and frankly I don't want to hear of that happening, ever. So, if there's any chance, even remotely—Well, if that's the main worry then how about switching to internal power, a battery or capacitor or some such, as soon as the route's been locked in—Of course it could work. And if we're only talking nanoseconds, well then all we need is nanoseconds—Good, that's what I'm here for. But I want people working on it right away—Yes, I want to see designs, sketches—Okay, and what about the lady herself, is she still being a nuisance? Still bothering us?—Oh, and why not?—Well, did we settle? Did she accept?—Right, sure. I see—Oh, come on, you're kidding, no?—Really?—Truly?—Oh, right. Huh—I hadn't—I guess so—Well, you know, keep an eye on her. Whatever you do don't go forgetting about her—No, I just mean it's the quiet ones you've got to worry about. At least when they're making a noise you know where you—Sure. And who can really say what she's cooking up—Well, let me know—Okay, good— That's good—What's next?—'

10. A Clear Path

'AND THEN I found myself out walking. Just aimlessly strolling. Out in the bamboo grove. I didn't want to stray too far from the house. It was cold. I didn't have my nightie on. I thought the bamboo would offer me some shelter. But when I looked up I saw all those tall swaying lines converging on the sky. Pointing towards it. The sky itself was overcast. And then I was rushing up into it. Along those lines. Into that sky. I hadn't wanted to go. Something took me. Something plucked me from my safety amid the bamboo and whooshed me into the air. But it was all wrong. I hadn't requested a transfer. I wasn't wearing the proper clothes. I wasn't wearing anything at all. And here I was now moving through cloud at this incredible speed. I was a sort of mist. The cloud clung to me. It tried to hold me to itself. It tried to tear me away from myself. But I was travelling too fast. I had already travelled thousands of miles. I couldn't see anything below me. It was hazy. Very dark. A sort of fuzzy dimness. But I had a strong sense of there being water. Somewhere far below me. A huge expanse. Limitless. I began to fear that as a cloud I'd be dropped into it. Precipitated into it. That I'd be tossed naked into the middle of that black ocean and it would suck me all the way under. But I was going too fast even for the water. For all those sucking depths of water. Though the land when it came would be worse.

And now I felt something pushing me downwards. I wasn't falling. I was being forced. Forced right out of the sky. And all over the earth were spots of red. Tiny red pinpricks. I was being hurled now towards one of them. One small red painted circle on dusty concrete beside some big metal wheelie bins. It was on an industrial estate. I could see all the buildings growing suddenly very large and I could pick out the details of the wheelie bins and the tall wire fences and the silent machinery. But the red spot itself didn't grow. It remained fixed. It glistened. Whatever was throwing me out of the sky was trying to get me in that small circle. Like a high diver into a bucket. And it stung. It really stung as I smacked into the middle of that circle. All my organs jarred with the force of it. I could feel them yanked suddenly downwards within me. It made me feel really sick. I felt so sick and I couldn't move. Not with the fresh weight of myself. My unclouded self. My naked self. I had no idea where I was. Some huge business complex in some foreign land. Round the front of the buildings others would be arriving and going inside for their conference. But here I was still out in the rear lot. Cramped within my small red circle. It was raining. I was crying. Everything was wet. But I knew I had to get out of that circle quick because someone else would be wanting to use it and they'd crash right on top of me. They'd appear in the same tight space and they'd mingle with me. It took all my effort to get clear. I was crawling so slowly. Painfully slow. Like I was trying to command someone else's body to move by thought alone and I could hardly feel that other body as I could hardly feel myself. And all the time I had the fear of the other's arrival. It terrified me. It urged me onward. But once I was clear I was fine. Once my last toe was dragged out of that circle my own strength returned to me. Just like that. I felt real again. New. Even the rain didn't bother me. It was warm. Like showering. Though I couldn't linger. I had to get going or else I'd be late for the conference. But just as I began walking away I heard a squeaking and bumping and rolling from behind me. Turning around I saw that one of the big metal wheelie bins was moving. Four small boys were pushing it. Wheeling it creakily forward. They had painted it red. The very same glistening blood-red paint as the circle. And they were laughing. Snickering to each other. So I called out to them. *Hey!* I was really angry. I could feel the anger surging hot inside me. I was naked in the rain in a strange land but I didn't care. That anger was rising. It was getting nearer. It was about to explode in front of me. And these small snickering boys were pushing the wheelie bin right onto the circle. And I felt in that moment how someone else was surely on their way. This other person was hurtling in through the clouds having travelled for thousands of miles. Very soon they'd be here. And they'd collide with the bin. They'd be forced to occupy the same space as the bin. I shouted again. *Hey! You can't do that. That's really dangerous. That's illegal.* But the boys merely snickered and chattered and yelped with delight. They called back. *It's only a joke. It's just for fun.* They buoyed each other with their laughter. No. I moved closer to them. *It's not a joke. Someone could really get hurt. You need to move it right now.* They stepped back as I stepped forward. *Oh no no no. You're wrong. You're quite wrong there. We don't need to do anything.* They were careful to stay out of reach. And still that other person was getting nearer. Someone just like me was rapidly approaching. I was fuming. The rain steamed as it struck my skin. The boys were terrified as I loomed towards them. They feared my awful nakedness. I was going to grab them and clutch them and squeeze them into understanding just how serious this was. *I'll report you to the authorities. You'll all be put in jail. I can arrest you. Right here. A citizen's arrest. What are your names? Tell me where you live!* And they cowered. They looked at the sky behind me and they trembled. Because something was coming in fast. Something was very nearly here. And now the boys realised. Now they understood. But all too late. For nothing could be done any more. And when this something arrived there was a tearing and a screaming. A hollow metallic wailing filled the air. The boys scurried off in a panic. But I turned. I spun round. And I saw the glistening red wheelie bin had merged with another traveller. She was trapped inside it. She was bashing and pounding its walls from within. And the wheelie bin shuddered and wobbled and boomed. But the traveller couldn't get out. She was trying to breathe inside it with all the rubbish of the world choking her. She was so frightened. But I wasn't frightened. In that moment all the fear and anger had gone from me. I was so calm I was unable to move. I could only stand and stare with my arms limp by my sides. Then the traveller too stopped moving. She stopped wailing and booming. All the strength had gone out of her. All the life had gone out of her. And it was very quiet inside the bin. It was all so dark and cramped. Death felt very cramped and lonely. Everyone had run away. No one cared that I was even there. No one knew. I didn't matter any more. I had never mattered. And I could hear the sound of the rain on the lid of the wheelie bin. And I could hear my own slow breath and feel my own thick heartbeat. But inside I was calm. Death itself felt very calm.'

¶

Trisha's hands were tight round her coffee mug. She was leaning forward over it, her morning tangle of red hair in a curtain around it as she stared into its dreggy emptiness. Now she relaxed a little, and leant back in her chair, and brushed her hair away as she looked up.

'Is it—anything like that?'

On the opposite side of the table sat Shui-Lin, busily buttering a second crumpet while still finishing the first and sipping at moments from her own small cup of coffee. Her hair was in similar morning disarray, its short scruffy blackness sticking out at angles from where it had scrunched against her pillow. She shook her head in response to the question, making through her mouthful a vaguely negative sound.

Trisha frowned. 'What, not at all?'

'Not really.' Shui-Lin swallowed forcefully. 'No. You see, you don't have much of a sense of it, actually. A bit of dizziness, maybe. Like a swirl. Like standing too fast. You know? It takes the mind a moment to adjust to its new surroundings. That's all. I try to shut my eyes. It makes it a bit easier. But you can't always do it in time. It's just so fast. See?'

'What about the bins though? That bit really scared me. Don't you find that scary?'

Shui-Lin stood up, the last curl of crumpet poking from the side of her mouth. She carried her plate and cup to the sink and slid them into the soapy water. She shook her head again.

'Couldn't happen. You can't just block a red site like that. The satellites would detect it. And there are other sensors too. They'd know somehow. Something would pick it up. And then the transfer wouldn't take place.'

'But what about in the final moments? If there was a blockage in those last few tiny—'

The question was interrupted by Shui-Lin's laughter.

'Trisha. It happens so so fast. Just a split second. You know? Like, really fast.' She shrugged, smiling. 'There's just no possible way it—'

But Trisha wasn't smiling. She sat sullenly, gazing down once more into her empty coffee mug.

Shui-Lin came to stand beside her, putting her hands lightly on Trisha's head. And Trisha let her head flop sideways against Shui-Lin, allowing herself to be held, to be stroked.

'I'm sorry. I didn't mean—Are you okay? I'm sure it must have been scary. It did sound pretty bad. And I am sorry you had to go through it. But it really was just your imagination. You know that, right? Just your old fears making the most of themselves while you slept.'

Trisha's eyes were wet. 'It was just so very real. And I hate it. I hate that you do it. You go through it every day, like it's nothing. And I know, I do know. You have to. I get that. But I hate it. And I wish you didn't have to. I wish no one did. I wish—' She went quiet.

A moment's pause and Shui-Lin took up from where Trisha had left off.

'You wish you could go back?' She felt the head move very slightly beneath her hands. 'I know. It's alright.'

Trisha looked up suddenly, her eyes wide. 'I don't mean go back home. I hope you don't think that. That's not what I meant. Because—I can't anyway. Not any more. And I really am happy here. I'd never even want to leave. I only mean—'

'Yes, I know. It's okay.'

The hair stroking was resumed for a while in silence. Then Shui-Lin patted Trisha gently, decisively, and moved away.

'But I really do need to get ready now. You'll be okay, right? Have something to eat. You really should. You'll feel much better.'

Trisha nodded weakly. Shui-Lin hurried off upstairs.

¶

The shower was very hot. It steamed, filling the small space behind the white shower curtain. Shui-Lin stood motionless beneath the spray, her eyes shut. She took in the heat, feeling her blood rise to the surface of her skin, feeling it strain to release all that new energy.

She heard the bathroom door open. She felt the wash of air and the space around her enlarging momentarily, then the gentle tap of plastic touching plastic, and the creak of one thing taking another's weight.

'You really are pathetic.' Shui-Lin opened her eyes, squinting beneath the spray. 'Can't you leave me be for even one second?'

'I know, I know. But I needed to go. And then, also, I was just thinking—'

Shui-Lin sighed and began soaping the stiff bristles of her wash brush. 'I think you do a little too much thinking. I think that's part of the problem. But go on, tell me anyway. Tell me about this thinking.'

The voice beyond the shower curtain began at once.

'I was thinking how it's still so easy to remember the old days. You know? Even though that was like twenty years ago or something. And I know it's kind of cliché to say everything was simpler then, but it's true, isn't it? Everything was. The cable system was so much simpler. So much less of a fuss. I even remember the public booths. Always making sure you carried a few coins in your pocket to pay the fare. I was only a girl but I still remember it all. And all so clearly. Don't you?'

'Uh-huh.'

'You knew where you were then. You bought your ticket, you got in the booth, and you were away. It was solid. It was fixed. It was a one-off payment.'

'And it was expensive.'

'Sure, of course. It had to be. But you knew that and you accepted it. And you didn't have to use it if you— well, if you didn't have to. But now. What do we have now? When did you last even buy a ticket?'

'Actually, I made a payment only a week or so ago.'

'Oh, sure, for a subscription, to continue the service. But that's not really a ticket. It's not the same thing.'

'It's kind of the same. Like a season ticket.'

'But one that never ends. Just renewed, renewed, re-newed. You'll never not be paying for it. No one will. It just goes on and on forever.'

Shui-Lin shut off the water and reached for her towel as she stepped out over the high lip of the bath.

'I'm not sure I see the difference, Trish. What exactly are you getting at?'

'Well, don't you miss it? Not being tied in? Not being so chained to the rest of the world? Having options? Having control?'

'I have plenty of options.'

'Yeah, right. For your desired level of service, maybe. For upgrades. For add-ons.'

'Yup.' Shui-Lin rubbed her short scruffy hair dry. 'And I like it that way. Maybe you liked the reassurance of a ticket. But this way I'm in control. I choose how I want to use the service. And it is indeed a service. And I do use it. Every day. I get exactly what I pay for.'

'No. Not that. I mean, you actually *have* to. You see? You don't get a choice. Not a real choice.'

'Well, that's just life. I have to work. I have to *get* to work. How would things be if I didn't? We all have to get—'

Trisha glared at her.

Shui-Lin stopped for a moment. 'I'm sorry. I wasn't meaning that. You know I didn't mean that. I'm—' She nodded to the door. 'I'm going to go and get dressed now. I shall be exiting the bathroom. So, do you think you'll be okay in here? For a little while? All on your ownsome?'

Trisha gave no reply.

¶

In her bedroom Shui-Lin paused in front of her open wardrobe.

'Upgrades, huh?'

She stared at the options available. There were many. She could afford a great many. Tops and bottoms and gloves and shoes. They were good designs. They were stylish. She could mix and match. And they were barely distinguishable from how things used to be. The detailing was getting better and better with each new range released.

'No different from wearing an old suit. Not really. Just the standard acceptable attire. And if everybody else wears the same, or mostly the same, then—'

She made her selection, a forest-green jacket and black slacks. Except these were just the outer layers. The inner parts were the same with all combinations: a dark glossy skin-tight fabric that covered her body right up to the throat. She drew herself into the one part then fixed the other over the top, fastening each garment to the next with discreet wires so that everything she wore was linked up as one continuous unit. Even the short boots she pulled on had to be connected to the rest.

From her jacket pocket she drew a slim black box. She checked the readout. Three diodes were lit amber, but two were blinking red for *gloves* and *hood*. That was okay. She wouldn't put those on till she was fully ready to go.

Trisha came in and flopped onto the bed.

'I'm so bored.' She eyed Shui-Lin surreptitiously. 'So so so—bored.'

'No, you're not.' Shui-Lin didn't look back at her. She lifted two small rucksacks from the wardrobe, weighty for their size, one in navy blue, the other mauve. Both were made of the same coarsely woven fabric as the jacket and slacks, with the same gold-rimmed connector points, and fine colour-matched wires leading out from each of them. 'And don't think I'm calling in sick. Not for your sake. There's a meeting this afternoon. It's important. They've asked me to be present.'

'They need you to travel halfway round the world just to sit in on some dumb meeting?'

'If I'm not there. If I don't make that little effort to be there in person and our competitors do? You know how that'll look.'

'Yeah, yeah. I know.'

'And it's not *halfway round the world*.' Shui-Lin sniffed, rubbed her nose, and put the navy blue rucksack back in the wardrobe. 'It's barely a quarter. Anyway, the distance is irrelevant. It's the same however far you go. You know—the lightning principle, and all that.' She unfastened a pouch on the mauve rucksack and checked the readout within.

Trisha craned to look. 'Is it charged? I hope it's properly charged. What if it suddenly loses power?'

'It's got plenty. And it doesn't use much anyway. Not these days.'

Trisha rolled onto her back. She stared at the ceiling. She listened to the sound of rain on the rooftop. 'Well, I don't understand it. Seems like it would need an awful lot of power. You know, for something like that.'

'No. Not really. Not any more.' Shui-Lin sounded vague. She was looking for something, checking the drawers of her bedside table, checking under the bed itself. 'It's—a different sort of coding. Different sort of scan. It gets used to you. It, uh—utilises stored data. Monitors microchanges, fluctuations, etc. Then it only needs to—' She straightened. 'Look, I don't really understand it either. But it works. That's all that actually matters in the—' She squinted towards the bed. 'Trisha, have you seen my pen?'

Trisha sat up, then reached over to her own side of the bed and rummaged among the items on the table there. Turning back she held out a pen. It was smooth and white, with a strange ergonomic design that curved in the middle and bulbed outward at one end. From some angles it looked like a piece of plastic cutlery.

Shui-Lin took it from her.

'Have you been using this?'

'No.'

'Trisha, these are very expensive.'

'So?'

'So—' Shui-Lin put it into her bag. 'There are plenty of other pens you could use.'

Trisha flopped back pettishly onto the bed.

'Oh yes, don't be forgetting your regulation pen, and regulation notebook, and regulation calculator, and regulation lunchbox. Gotta get all the accessories. Gotta collect the whole set. God knows what might happen if you travelled with something in your pockets that wasn't manufactured by, and purchased directly from, our wise and propitious overlords.'

Shui-Lin ignored her and went to stand by the window, glancing out at the rain. From her pocket she once again took out the slim black box and ran her thumb over a notched wheel, scrolling through her list of saved destinations.

The voice that came from behind her was suddenly very soft.

'Shui-Lin?'

'Yes?'

'Don't you miss having long hair?'

Shui-Lin didn't answer. Rainwater was falling in a long broken curtain from the guttering. She could see a little patch of blue sky far out over the forest.

'I preferred you with long hair. It was so—you.'

'You know why I have it short.'

'I know. But your eyelashes must stick out beyond the hood too, occasionally, maybe, and *they* don't get chopped off. In any case, do you think that would actually happen to your hair? I mean, really?'

'I don't know. I don't think that's the reason anyhow. It's just more—convenient.'

'But don't you miss it?'

'Everybody has short hair.' She shrugged. 'It doesn't matter. It's easier that way.'

'Shui-Lin?'

'Yes?'

'Do you resent me being here?'

'No.'

'Because I do. Every day. When you're not here. I feel guilty.'

'I know you do. It's alright.'

'Because I don't contribute. Not financially.'

'You don't need to. I make more than enough.'

'And I'm sorry. Sorry for how I whinge on sometimes. I really am.'

'It's okay.'

'I just get really scared.'

'It's okay. I understand. It did sound pretty horrible, your dream. I didn't mean to make light of it. I'm—just a little rushed. You know how it is.'

Trisha didn't reply.

The blue of the sky was spreading. The hazy sheets of rain were thinning. Shui-Lin put on the mauve rucksack and plugged it in to the rest of her suit. There was a fine high-pitched tone, barely audible, and her skin prickled beneath the clingy inner fabric. On her tiny display four amber lights now showed, but the two reds were still blinking.

Shui-Lin drew the tight black sock of the hood up over her head. It covered her ears and mouth and nose like a balaclava, leaving only a slit for her eyes. Over her hands she slipped two gloves of that same smooth material. She sat down on the edge of the bed. Trisha was facing away from her.

Shui-Lin leaned forward and kissed Trisha's mess of soft red hair, the hood's dark film holding back the brief press of her lips. There was a fine beeping from inside the green jacket.

Trisha turned about as Shui-Lin slid the black box from her pocket. They looked at it together. Now all the lights were amber. They were blinking in unison.

'How long?'

'About five minutes. Probably a little more.'

'And that's what you get for the premium package? Five minutes?'

Shui-Lin nodded.

'Not exactly instant service.'

Within the hood's narrow window Shui-Lin's eyes creased a little at their corners.

'Best not to be too hasty with these things.'

She withdrew from the room and went downstairs.

¶

Outside the rain was still falling, though thinned now to near nothing.

Over the black balaclava Shui-Lin pulled a second hood, the jacket's own dark green hood. It hung stiffly forward, shading her eyes. As with the body of the jacket it was mostly decorative, though it did help keep off the last light drops of rain. The weather itself made no difference to travelling. Shui-Lin simply preferred not to get too wet.

A narrow path of decking led over the lawn and into the bamboo grove. At the end was a small clearing, into which Shui-Lin now stepped.

She positioned herself at the very centre. She looked up through the bamboo stems. They swayed gently, their long lines converging, all pointing towards a narrow circle of sky.

On the display of the black box the blinking amber lights had each turned to a steady green. The box beeped once more.

Shui-Lin took a deep breath. She closed her eyes—and waited.

11. Further, More

FROM WHERE the two men were sitting, high on the side of the bluestone mountain, the desert plain looked empty and flat. It looked like it stretched all the way to the far horizon, as though there was nothing but that flatness continuing right over the rest of the world. Except, if they strained their eyes through the distant haze, what they had at first taken for a long smooth curve showed very faintly to be a jagged grey ridge, marking where the ring of mountains once again began.

It wasn't much of a camp, they'd merely stopped for a breather. They'd shucked off their heavy packs and unfolded a couple of lightweight collapsible chairs. From a chilled inner pocket one man now drew two bottles of beer. He cracked off the caps, letting them fall to the blue-grey dust at his feet, then passed an open bottle to his companion.

The two men sat back contentedly. They gazed out over the plain. There wasn't much to look at but the vastness of that empty space of air, pressing the desert flat. There wasn't much to hear but the non-stop chirping and buzzing of insects, or the occasional unseen scuttle of a lizard. And yet, every so often, they thought they could discern voices, faint, thin, floating up on the breeze from the desert floor. Voices like workmen calling over a loudhailer. They couldn't make out any words, the distance must have been too great, the signal of those voices getting broken by the wind and arriving in patches.

The light, when they saw it, wasn't all that spectacular. Just a gleam out on the plain. A mere spot of brightness that lifted, slowly at first, then gradually faster, up into the thickness of the air, past the ragged line of the horizon, and on into the clear blue of the sky. By then of course they'd heard it: the muffled rumble of powerful thruster engines, rolling and booming up from the middle of the plain, and then from the air itself, a giant ripping sound, as though the very sky was being torn open, not quickly, but consistently, definitively, leaving a long grey seam of vapour where the rip had formed.

They saw too the dust spreading out from the launch point, and a short while later felt a gentle wave of warm moist air waft up and over them, carrying on it the tang of something metallic, an iron bite that caught in the back of the throat.

The two men sipped from their bottles. One of them began nodding enthusiastically.

'Man! I mean, whew! Now, Jake, that sure is something special, ain't it? I love seeing them do that. All that power. That muscle. Makes you kinda shivery to think about it.'

'Sure does, Pete.' The other man nodded as well, but more slowly. 'Makes you proud too though, don't it? Like, how far we've come? How far we've still to go?'

'Whew!' Pete sipped from his bottle then pointed the neck out at the rocket, now little more than a fine white dot arcing out into the blue. 'And them getting another satellite up there? Yup, that makes good sense. I mean, sure, some folks would say as you don't need it. Like it's a waste or something. But I reckon you can't have too many, right? Makes the whole process more accurate. Like, say the whole sky was full of them? Like a giant intricate web, dotted all over the sky? That'd be kinda magnificent. That'd be better for everyone.'

'Not sure that's actually possible, Pete. But yeah, I get what you mean.'

They gazed at the sky a while, the air still full of a gentle grumbling, like departing thunderclouds.

Pete closed one eye and held his bottle out at arm's length, its base to the middle of the plain, then: 'Ptcheeeoow!' And the bottle lifted off slowly into the sky in a gentle arc back towards Pete's lips, where it was duly tipped upwards.

Jake smiled. 'Not that this one's a satellite, mind. This one's going all the way. This one's headed right to the moon.'

'Whoa! Really? How can you tell?'

Jake shrugged. 'Oh, you get to hearing things. You know. People talk.'

'Oh, right. Sure.' Pete squinted up into the sky. He could still see the rocket, but not the moon. 'I wonder what they want with that old rock anyway. I was always told there ain't nothing on the moon now but faded flags and footprints.'

'Not *on* it, no. Not at the surface. But *under* it.' Jake grinned. 'The moon's rich, Pete. Didn't you know? It's got all the minerals we'll ever need, just up there, forever floating above our heads. And no worries about digging them out, either. No compulsory purchase orders. No stubborn old lady refusing to budge over her tiny postage stamp of land.'

Pete nodded. 'Whoa—rich, huh? That makes you think.' He continued nodding for a moment, then he lifted his beer bottle close to his eye and looked through its curved sides at the departing rocket. He could only just see the glimmer of the engines through the distortion of brown glass, and only then if he held himself very still. He lowered the bottle. 'How do you suppose they're gonna bring all that stuff back? That's gotta be real heavy. Sure would be expensive too. You'd think it'd be a helluva lot easier digging it out down here than all the way up there.'

'They ain't carting it back by the rocket-load, Pete! No, no. They'll be setting up one of those transporter stations. Up there on the moon. That's where they're off to now.' He tipped his own bottle in the general direction of the rocket. 'They're gonna go build a real big one. Then they just whizz back the goods as and when they've got a full bucket. No great problem. No extra expense.'

Pete rocked back on his chair. 'Oh man, now that's clever. That's real genius right there.' He looked doubtful for a moment. 'How do you come to know all this, Jake? I ain't heard it on the news. And you'd think they'd mention a thing like that. If it was official, like.'

'Been rumours for a while. And rumours don't come out of nowhere. But you know how it is—they gotta at least try and keep it secret.'

'Right, right. In case someone steals their ideas.' Pete smiled again. 'But once it's up and running, then— bam! Just like that. All those riches will start pouring in. It's gonna make the world wealthy all over again.' He nodded. 'Yeah, that does sound pretty sensible.'

'Sure is. And it's the same with the workers, too. Cos, you know, it ain't much fun being on the moon for so long. You go all flaky. Wobbly. Your body kinda gives up on you. Your bones turn to mush.'

'Right, right. So—they'll be using like robots or something?'

'What? No. Well—yeah, maybe they'll use machines and that, of course, for digging out the stuff itself. But no, it'll be guys like you and me who'll do the steering, the actual operating of those machines.'

'Right, like until just before their bones turn to mush, and then they come back. Whew! That's tough. I mean, I wouldn't wanna be those guys. I sure hope the job pays well.'

'No, Pete. That's not what—' Jake took off his cap, rubbing at his brow with the heel of his palm. 'They'll be sending the workers up in shifts, see? You know, via the transporter? So, each one spends just a short while up on the moon, does a bit of digging, comes back to recuperate, and then after a few weeks when they've got their strength back, up they go again for another stint. And sure, I guess they'll be paid a good amount for it. Or a half-decent wage, in any case.'

Pete sat forward in his seat, staring out over the plain. He rolled his bottle between his hands then tipped it slowly onto its side, watching the shape of the liquid change within. He tried to get that slowly stretching surface as close as he could to the lip without spilling it. He tilted the bottle with great care. But because of the neck's narrowing, the liquid gave a sudden surge and a measure glugged out and splashed into the dust before Pete could right the bottle again. Only a small amount was lost. Nothing to be concerned about. Not in proportion to how much the bottle had held.

Pete sniffed. 'Well, even so, I guess I sure wouldn't like to be the first guy that tries *that* trip. You know, after they get the big transporter up and running.'

Jake nodded. 'True enough, true enough. That's a mighty long way to the moon. And it won't be good thick air they'll be zipping through. Sending minerals is one thing, sure, but a person? Well—'

'You'd think they'd test it. You know, before sending up the rocket? Before building the whole thing. You'd think they'd wanna make sure first.'

'Oh, they did. Well, kind of. As close as they could anyhow. They sent a guy right round the world. They hopped him from satellite to satellite. They had to rig it up all special. But there was that guy. They did it.'

'Whoa—that had to be some trip! Poor guy musta felt real dizzy.'

'Sure he musta been dizzy. They had to send him round like a dozen times, all in one go. You know, to simulate the full distance to the moon? And I think they were pretty worried too, cos of all that curving. Cos he'd've been going at quite a lick, see, so they were worried some of his particles might like fling off into space? At least going to the moon'll be more or less direct. But in any case—things seemed to work out alright.'

'So, how long did it take him, end to end?'

'I dunno.' Jake shrugged. 'Say, like—five minutes or something?'

'Sheesh, that's kinda pretty slow, actually. Don't you reckon? That's a long time to be on the move like that. A long time to be, you know, not altogether yourself.'

'Yeah, musta been all those junctions on the way. Probably slowed things down a fair bit. I'm guessing the moon trip will be a lot smoother.'

Pete tried tipping his bottle again. The level was lower this time and the angle seemed to change more rapidly, so Pete took extra care, watching as the liquid neared the neck. But the level was now so low that the bottle was past horizontal before there was that sudden surge and another big glug was lost, swallowed quickly by the dry earth.

Pete winced as he righted the bottle. It felt like he'd lost just as much on the second go as the first. He looked up at the sky. He couldn't see any sign of the rocket's engines any more, only the long curve of its vapour trail, still hanging in the air.

'Do you think they'll manage it?'

'Sure they will. They wouldn't be trying if they didn't think it was possible. Look at all of what they've achieved so far.'

'I know, I know.' Pete bobbed. 'But I was just thinking. Like, maybe they should've waited a while longer? You know, just to be sure.'

'What?'

Pete stared at the ground between his feet. 'Well, just seems like all through history someone's always got to be the first to do this, or the first to discover that, or the first to get to some hard-to-reach place, and get all the way back home again. And they take all these fantastic risks? Just so as it's them that can be the first? And often people die along the way, because they're all trying too hard, or else not hard enough, or they don't have the right sort of kit. But like, whenever I heard such stories

I always used to think, well, why didn't they just wait a little while longer? Like why not get it all worked out first, make sure it's all real safe, make sure you got kit that won't give up of a sudden. You know, why not make it easy for yourself? Because it's like they're always in such a rush, and so they always make mistakes, things they hadn't thought of till they happen. So I always thought, like, if they just waited a while, whoever was first *then*, well, they'd still be first. Just a bit later on. And I don't suppose it matters much who that person is, right?'

'Oh, come on, Pete. I think you're missing the point. If they all just hung around till it got easy, well now—where's the fun in that? And what would happen to the journey itself? All those happy accidents along the way? Those mistakes? Those little challenges? Aren't those the sorts of things that make life just that little bit more exciting?'

'I guess. Maybe. I don't know.'

'And what about all the little extras? The unlooked-for bonuses. Like climbing this here mountain and us getting such a great view of the rocket launch. I don't suppose anyone else got such a view. And sure, we could have put all our resources into watching just that launch, but hey, we didn't even know it was happening! It was an accident. A good accident. We'd not have seen it without this forward push, this drive to reach the top. And we'd not've been pushing to get to the top if we weren't getting paid to. If it wasn't our job to. You see? And we're climbing it now so that others don't have to. We're doing the hard work. The good work.'

Pete nodded slowly, squinting at the dust. He put his beer bottle to his lips and tipped it back, but the bottle was empty. He held it up to the light and stared at it, as though its emptiness was some kind of trick. Then he upended it and, gripping it by the neck, hurled it back down the slope of the mountain where it smashed against a large boulder and splintered into hundreds of sparkling pieces.

Jake did the same with his own bottle and the two men sat for a moment listening to the short-lived echoes rebounding off the rocks. For a while the chirping and buzzing of insects was silenced. Everything was silent in the aftershock of the smashed bottles. Then, slowly, gradually, the chirping and buzzing resumed.

Jake stood and stretched. 'We'd best get going. I want to be up there before sundown so as we can get it done quick and get on home straight after.' He began folding up his chair to stow in his pack, motioning for Pete to follow suit. 'And check your cans while you're about it.'

'What for?'

'For breakages, of course. Last time I was up this way the guy I came with spilled his cans. The plastic had split in his pack and when he took it out it broke open and spilled all over the place. Made a real mess. We hadn't even started work. Red everywhere. Glistening all over the rocks. And you can't just be scrubbing that stuff off. It's super tough. Damned expensive too. They had to send in a special team for the clean-up. They had to blast it off the rocks with high-pressure hoses. Real costly getting all that gear up here. But they had to. Who knows what the satellites would've made of a big ugly splodge like that. Now, I'm not saying you're as clumsy as the other fella, but you did put your pack down pretty hard when we stopped.'

Pete dutifully, cautiously, checked the cans of red paint he'd been tasked with carrying. Then he hoisted the heavy pack onto his shoulders and the two men trudged on up the mountain.

'Jake?'

'Yup?'

'So, I was wondering—what exactly do they need all them moon minerals for?'

'Why, Pete! For all the new machines, of course! All these new technologies? You see, they all use up a lot of resources. A lot of energy.'

Out over the plain the rocket's vapour trail was dispersing. Its long curve had been growing slowly fatter and now parts of it were fading in the high desert air, just as other parts were floating away as small puffy clouds, breaking up the line.

'So, I guess they've gotta build more machines on the moon so as they can send more minerals back to build more machines down here and so send more people to the moon?'

'Now you're getting it! Yup, that's the forward push. A lot of work still to do, of course. A lot of work. And all for the good of folks like you and me. All for the good of mankind.'

The two walkers picked their way with care up over the blue-grey rocks. The sun had put their side of the mountain in shadow. It made the going easier. The sky was still bright. The rocket was nowhere to be seen.

'Plus, once they've got it all up and running, they can build whatever they like up there. Whole cities could be sent up flat-packed, just like that, and put together in a jiffy.'

There were voices coming up from the desert plain. Little fragments of voices. Metallic voices. Their calls intermittent, their words indistinct. They buzzed and chirped as they rose on the warm mountain air.

'Cities on the moon, Jake? Why'd they wanna do a thing like that?'

'Oh, I dunno, Pete. I'm just saying as they could, is all. You know? Just saying as they could.'